I live in South Yorkshire. I left school when I was fifteen to work in general labouring jobs. Whatever else I was doing, I was always writing poems, short stories, novels.

I was encouraged to write while at school by two teachers, Mrs. Tooth and Miss. Stafford. Taking their advice has given me endless hours of pleasure. I also enjoy walking, gardening, eating out, real ale and music.

BETTY

J.C. Smith

BETTY

Vanguard Press

A CIP catalogue record for this title is
available from the British Library.

ISBN 978 1 784653 74 3

*Vanguard Press is an imprint of
Pegasus Elliot MacKenzie Publishers Ltd.*
www.pegasuspublishers.com

First Published in 2018

**Vanguard Press
Sheraton House Castle Park
Cambridge England**

Printed & Bound in Great Britain

This book is for my parents, who told me the stories.

Chapter One.

A scream rent the evening air. Everyone looked up to see the girl's body sliding around the red chute hurtling towards the floor, where her boyfriend caught her and lifted her to her feet.

"Again," she said breathlessly laughing at his concerned look. "Again." She ran off to the man with the leather pouch to pay for another ride. The helter-skelter was doing good business today. Flashing lights of red, yellow and gold. Barrel organ music, and the smell of steam engines. The sound of bells being rung, the thump of a sledge hammer on leather. Screams and shouting from the milling crowds. The smell of chestnuts roasting over charcoal fires. Painted horses circling on the roundabouts. The people sliding down the helter-skelter, screaming to friends below as they speed earthwards, laughing as they go. All the fun of the fair.

Betty watched the people jostling each other as they moved from stall to stall, dressed in their Sunday best, carrying toffee apples and candy floss. Some with rag dolls, clutched tightly under their arms, or carrying goldfish in jam jars. Hard won prizes to be carried home and bragged about for a few days before the pressure of work returned and the fair became a distant memory. But for now there were the ghost shows, steam yachts, the switchbacks, the coconut shies; there were so many things to see and do, it was work that was the distant memory while the fair was in town.

The moving mass of humanity that was the Goose Fair crowd moved as one past Betty's stall. It appeared at times as if it were a single entity guided by some unseen force leading it this way and that; never allowing it to stop, but forever moving it from one stall to another in noisy revelry.

Betty glanced to her left, towards the stall where Mrs Cohen was busy selling a bracelet to a giggling girl in a blue gingham skirt, white blouse, and cardigan, her boyfriend by her side, with only eyes for her, dressed in his best charcoal grey suit, white shirt and blue tie, matching her skirt. She could have anything on the stall, Betty thought, at this moment, he wouldn't care. The sale completed, the couple ran off quickly disappearing into the molten crowd. She laughing and looking at her wrist, and him looking only at her.

Mrs. Cohen was Betty's employer, or to be perfectly honest, she employed Betty's mother as a cleaner. She had been a stallholder when the fair was more of a market than it was now. She told Betty tales of the geese, from where the goose fair got its name, arriving with black, tar-covered feet in droves. The tar was to make sure their delicate feet would stand the journey. Because they had to walk all the way from their respective farms, there was no other way to transport them. But now it was more a fair for fun rather than commerce. There were still a few stalls selling things but the days of selling livestock were long gone. Only the name remained to remind people of its origins. Whenever the fair was in town Mrs Cohen encouraged Betty to come along and run the coconut shy. Mrs. Cohen could quite easily have run both stalls herself, but she enjoyed Betty's company, and it gave her a break in the long days behind the counter. Betty had been coming to the fair since she was thirteen, she was now sixteen and felt like an old hand at the game. Her job was simple. She had a bucket of wooden balls, and when a customer came she sold him three balls for a farthing. If by any stroke of luck he managed to knock a coconut down she gave him the coconut he'd hit, and replaced it with a new one from under the counter, while calling out as loudly as possible that the shy had a winner and pointing to the hapless chap, who would be blushing and trying desperately to disappear into the milling throng.

She loved it when she got a winner, because then, for a while she had a lot of customers, and she enjoyed being busy. Sometimes she got a little bored just standing there, her feet feeling the cold from the grass beneath. Occasionally she would shout 'Roll up, roll up', but she was embarrassed shouting out; it was she then who was blushing, but as Mrs. Cohen said, it was all part of the job. So she did it when she got bored, but only then! At the moment she was enjoying watching the crowd queueing for the Helter Skelter. No sooner had they slid down from the top of the yellow tower, with the chute spiralling down the outside in red, than they were picking up their mats and joining the queue for another go. Betty promised herself a slide before she went home that night, it looked such good fun.

Just then, as she made her promise to herself, someone arrived and she had a customer. She gave him his three balls and stood to one side while he threw them. He didn't get anywhere near, much to the amusement of his friends.

"Come on then, boys. Let's see you do better. Give them all some balls Betty. Come on then boys. I'll take their money, you hand out the balls." Mrs. Cohen shamed all the boy's friends into having a go themselves. Soon quite a crowd had gathered to watch the friendly rivalry between the group as each egged on one against the other, or jeered a miss. Soon a second set of balls were required and the boys again were challenging each other. The coconuts rocked but none fell. The boys spent a penny each but no one won anything. By now a greater part of the queue from the helter-skelter, drawn by the raucous cries from the group of lads, was calling for balls, and so for the better part of an hour Betty and her employer were very busy indeed. There was much friendly banter from the crowd, one man accusing Mrs. Cohen of having glued the coconuts down. Mrs. Cohen with a feigned look of hurt and disgust at such effrontery, sat on the edge of the counter and swung her legs over causing her challenger to step back, much to the amusement of the crowd. Taking the man's own missiles from his hand, she, using all three balls, hit the same nut with each ball and knocked it down, to a great cheer from the crowd, and much jeering of the man when he tried to claim the coconut saying he'd paid for the balls. Eventually Mrs. Cohen gave him three more balls, with much shaking of her head and feigned, tut-tutting, causing more cheering from the crowd. But now the man was under so much pressure from the onlookers that he fared little better than he had on his first throw, so as the crowd began to disperse she gave her foil a coconut as a consolation prize for being such a good sport. As he went away he was telling anyone who'd listen how he came by it. "You'd think he'd won it," grinned Mrs. Cohen winking at Betty. "He's better than shouting 'Roll up' Eh Betty?" Betty nodded. She'd seen Mrs Cohen pull the same trick many times before and she still didn't know how she did it. When she asked, Mrs Cohen would put her index finger against her nose and just nod. "It's knowing the right nut," she'd say enigmatically. This ploy brought a fresh group of customers and Mrs. Cohen had now engineered another rush which lasted another half hour. When it died down she said, "I think we'll have a cuppa. Don't you Betty? I think we deserve one."

Betty took her cue and slipped behind the green and white striped tarpaulin which acted as roof and windbreak over the two stalls. Here, behind the stalls they kept a box which contained sandwiches and fruit, apples today, and all the makings for a cup of tea. Some of the other stallholders brought vacuum flasks, others just brought cold tea in bottles, but Mrs. Cohen liked freshly brewed tea so she had a spirit stove, a small kettle, bottle of fresh milk bought that morning and a caddy of tea. No sugar. She didn't take sugar, so Betty had learned to drink tea without it when working on the stall. In fact now she preferred it without. There were also two canvas chairs which they would use to sit in when they 'had a minute' as Mrs. Cohen said during quiet times over the course of the day. Just now though they drank their tea at the counter when Betty had made it. The fair was getting busy. It was just after seven in the evening, and a lot of people were walking down to have a look around after work. From now until about nine p.m. would be particularly busy, and tomorrow, Saturday, would be busier still. And so it proved, by the time their cups were empty both stalls were busy and remained so until close to ten p.m. Mrs Cohen was very pleased with the day's takings and gave Betty a shiny sixpence as a bonus. So Betty was pleased too. As they cleared up, getting things ready for the following day Mrs. Cohen said, "I think you've got an admirer. In fact I'm sure you have." She grinned at Betty's discomfiture.

"Me?" Betty blushed, not knowing why.

"Certainly you. He's not coming to look all cow eyes at me is he?" laughed Mrs. Cohen.

"But who do you mean? Cow eyes." She tried to laugh it off.

"That ginger-haired boy. The one with the gang who came early on. You remember?"

Betty shook her head. She could remember the rush. But individuals she couldn't bring to mind. It was just a sea of faces to her.

"Come on, don't tell me you can't remember. He would only take balls from you. He was so busy looking at you he was lucky to hit the side of the stall. He never hit a nut all night. All his mates were laughing at him. Then when they left

13

he came back on his own pretending to be in the queue for the helter-skelter until his friends found him again. Then he had to pay and go down the slide. Don't tell me you never saw him. The poor lad, he was mooning about all night and you never noticed him. If he knew he'd probably hang himself." She laughed and slapped Betty, who was still blushing, beetroot red, playfully on the shoulder. "Come on, let's go home. It's going to be another long day tomorrow."

They set off to Mrs. Cohen's car. She was the only person that Betty knew who owned one, and Betty loved just to sit in it. When she rode in it she felt like royalty. It was such a treat. She was always amazed that Mrs. Cohen never seemed to feel the same way about it.

"You really can't remember the lad?" Mrs. Cohen carried on where she'd left off. Much to Betty's chagrin.

Betty shook her head and climbed into the Rover.

"Poor lad. I'll scour the papers tomorrow for his obituary. On your head be it." They drove off into the now dark September night laughing. The sky was full of stars, the moon was almost full, brightening the road in front of them. Betty had a shiny sixpence in her pocket and according to Mrs. Cohen, who was still laughing as she drove through the dark Nottinghamshire night, away from the Goose Fair site, she had a secret admirer. Life felt good for Betty at sixteen.

It was September 1912, under two years to go to the event that would change all their lives forever.

CHAPTER TWO.

Saturday dawned all too quickly, and Betty, still tired from the day before walked to the Cohen's house with her mother. It was unusual for Betty's mum to work on Saturday but she occasionally did when the Cohens had dinner guests, so Betty thought nothing of it.

Mrs. Cohen was waiting for them at the door, but when she Saw Betty's mother she told Betty to wait in the car, and the pair went together into the house. Betty assumed that Mrs. Cohen was showing her mother the work she needed her to do and thought no more about it. Betty busied herself looking at the walnut facia in the car and wondering what all the dials and switches were for that were set into it. She imagined herself driving down the road with the window open and her hair blowing freely in the warm summer wind. The sound of the car door opening and Mrs. Cohen entering the car broke her reverie. Mrs. Cohen started the car and turned it around on the gravel drive, before driving out of the gates and turning onto the road towards the fairground site. She was unusually quiet and Betty thought she must be as tired as she herself was. They drove for a couple of miles or so before Mrs. Cohen spoke. "Well, Betty this is going to be a big day I think. So let's make it the best one yet." She smiled across at her bemused passenger.

Betty just nodded, not understanding what Mrs. Cohen was talking about. She is just tired, Betty thought.

When they got there they readied the stalls, Betty making sure all the wooden balls were in the two buckets under the counter, and refilling the cups that the coconuts stood in, where necessary, with sawdust, and setting the coconuts straight in them. Once she was satisfied her stall was right she passed through the little gate between the two stalls and helped Mrs. Cohen with hers. Hanging the cheap gold necklaces and bracelets on hangars, to show them to their best advantage. Then stretching others around headless pasteboard necks on a shelf along the back of the stall. When they were both satisfied with their work Betty made tea, and they then sat in their respective canvas chairs waiting for the gates to open at noon. Mrs. Cohen seemed a little preoccupied. She wasn't her normal garrulous self. Betty wondered if there was anything wrong, and was considering how to ask the question when Mrs. Cohen spoke.

"I wonder if your young man will turn up today." She grinned mischievously.

"I haven't got a young man. As well you know," blushed Betty.

"It's not through want of him trying though." She nodded sagely. She seemed back to her normal self. Betty put her earlier taciturn mood down to tiredness, she wasn't getting any younger Betty thought. Soon the crowds were spilling through the gates and they were back at their respective counters as if they'd never been away.

Both stalls did good business but as evening arrived it seemed as if every beau wanted to buy his girl some token because soon Betty was helping out Mrs. Cohen as the coconut shy became quiet.

Mrs. Cohen didn't just sell jewellery, she bought old gold and silver too. Mr. Cohen was a jeweller and made use of anything they bought at the fair, in his trade.

Eventually things quietened down and Betty managed to make a well-earned cup of tea. As they enjoyed it Mrs. Cohen nudged Betty hard in the ribs, and nodded towards the helter-skelter. Betty histrionically rubbed her ribs while Mrs. Cohen laughed and nodded theatrically again in the same direction. Through the gap between the helter-skelter and the galloping horses she could see the gang of boys who'd spent a long time the night before unsuccessfully trying to win a coconut heading their way. "Here they come. I don't see your boy though."

Betty just tutted and shook her head.

"Oh! He's there. I couldn't see his ginger hair, he's got a black cap on," smiled Mrs. Cohen as Betty involuntarily turned to look.

"You are interested then," she called, as Betty blushed and the boys arrived.

Betty didn't answer but she had to admit to herself that she was. The boy was tall a little gangly, and sunburned. The sort of colour you get from spending long hours outdoors. He had blond hair, Which Mrs. Cohen insisted on calling ginger, and large brown eyes. Betty couldn't believe she hadn't noticed him before. He did tend to hang around at the back of the crowd, and he didn't look at her directly. He tended to look at the ground when she spoke to him. But there was no doubt that she found him attractive.

Mrs. Cohen was watching their interaction with great interest. Every time Betty looked at her she nodded and pulled a"What do you think then?" kind of face. Betty did her best to ignore her and not to laugh, but she did find it difficult. She handed out the balls to the boys. They started as they had the evening before, with three balls each. After the first throw the rivalry surfaced, each one egging the others on, until they'd all thrown a dozen balls each, all to no avail. No one had even rattled a coconut never mind coming close to unseating one. They began to lose interest and slowly drift off. It appeared that one of the boys had a friend who was going to fight the fairground champion in the boxing booth, and they were all heading off in that direction. Only the ginger-haired boy seemed reluctant to go. Betty didn't know what to do. He was just turning to follow his friends, still in two minds when Mrs. Cohen shouted, "Come on, my lad. One last go."

By now the others were out of earshot, lost amongst the milling crowd, flashing lights and barrel organ music. One of the group was just visible near the test your strength machine, where he appeared to be considering having a go. The others had disappeared altogether.

He mumbled something neither of them could hear, but didn't follow his friends. Mrs. Cohen placed the three balls she was holding on the counter.

"Roll up, roll up. Come on roll up," she called to the crowd milling past. "Watch this game, young man, win a coconut. Come on now. If he wins he doesn't pay for his throw. I can't be fairer than that, can I?"

She'd drawn quite a crowd with this offer, and the boy was crimson up to his cap. Mrs. Cohen knew how to draw a crowd, Betty thought. But she felt sorry for the boy knowing he was only in this predicament because of her. She tried to quiet Mrs. Cohen, but she was just now getting into her stride. "Roll up. Come on, me lad! Show 'em how it's done."

One man stepped forward and paying a halfpenny took six balls, only hitting one coconut with them.

"This lad can do better than that." She pointed at the enamoured boy, still red to the roots of his hair, much to the chagrin of the first thrower.

The boy, unable to stand the chiding any more, stepped forward and picked up the wooden balls Mrs. Cohen had laid on the counter for him. She walked the length of the counter and stood at the opposite side to her own stall. "Right lad, give it your best shot." She said leaning on the counter and looking past the boy into the crowd that had now gathered.

He'd put his farthing on the counter when he picked up the balls, but Mrs. Cohen never looked at it.

"Never mind this lot." She waved disdainfully at the gathering. Someone jeered good-naturedly, "Come on then," she jeered back. "Have a go if you think you can do any better."

The heckler, chastened, stepped forward and laid his money down. Immediately picking up the balls he began to throw wildly. Mrs. Cohen nodded to the boy and said something to him quietly. He took careful aim, and missed completely. Just below him the second thrower was lining up his last shot, he threw, missing. Seconds later the boy threw and a coconut hit the ground. The boy couldn't believe it. He looked agog. "We have a winner, and he's still got a ball left," Mrs. Cohen called, "and as I promised he keeps his money."

She passed the nut to Betty to give to the boy, while she handed out balls to members of the gathered crowd who thought they could do as well as him.

"Here you are," Betty said, handing him his prize.

"I don't know how I did that," he stammered, with obvious pride. "I've never won anything before." He said, looking lovingly at the bristly brown object in his hands. "I don't even know what to do with it."

Betty pointed out the darker spots on the top of the nut and explained how to drain the milk from it, "then just break it, carefully so's not to damage the kernel or get it dirty and eat it. They're delicious."

"I suppose you've eaten lots of them?" he questioned.

"I've had some. Yes. But not a lot." It was difficult to know what to say. "What did she say to you just before you threw?" Betty tried to change the subject.

He shrugged. "She said, throw at the same time as him. No one will be watching you then." He shrugged again. "It worked." He grinned.

Betty was desperately trying to think of the next topic. She knew he wouldn't carry on talking. She could see someone at Mrs. Cohen's stall but she was still taking money on the coconut shy because Betty was talking to the lad and he didn't seem to want to leave. He was tongue-tied also. They just stood looking at each other.

Walter, are you coming? Robbie's fighting next." One of the gang had come back and was calling to him from the test your strength machine.

Walter waved the coconut at his friend who looked suitably impressed.

"I'll have to go." He blushed.

Betty nodded. "Walter?"

He blushed even more, and nodded.

"I'm Betty." She held out her hand. He took it and shook it as he was turning away.

"Will you be here tomorrow?"

She nodded, "In the evening. Remember its Sunday." She looked at the ground now. The fairground only opened in the evenings on Sundays.

"See you after church then." He called back bravely over his shoulder as he ran off grinning to join his friend.

Betty stood and watched him disappear amongst the throng.

"What's his name then?"

Betty jumped she'd been miles away and hadn't heard Mrs. Cohen approach.

"Walter," she answered self-consciously, not looking at her employer.

"You'll have to watch him you know. He'll soon have a ring on that finger. He's got it bad has that one."

"Mrs. Cohen." Betty couldn't look at her, she could feel the heat in her face as she stared at the grass beneath her feet.

"You mark my words, girl." She nodded knowingly.

"How did he win that coconut anyway?" Betty changed the subject.

Mrs. Cohen tapped the side of her nose and winked as usual. "Tricks of the trade, girl. Tricks of the trade." She strode purposefully towards her jewellery stall before her customer got away, grinning devilishly over her shoulder as she went.

Betty grinned back and shouted out to the crowd to roll up, which they did for the rest of the evening. Until ten o'clock both stalls were busy and there was little time for any banter.

At about nine o'clock they saw Walter's gang go past with a badly beaten boy in their midst and Betty surmised it was the one they'd been going to watch at the boxing booth. She didn't see Walter with them, although she scoured the group for sign of him. She felt disappointed and didn't quite know why.

After clearing everything away and leaving the stalls ready for the Sunday evening Mrs. Cohen drove Betty home. The journey was quiet, Mrs. Cohen seemed preoccupied. It was strange after the jocularity of the earlier evening. Betty again began to wonder if there was anything wrong at home, but Betty herself had other things on her mind and she was glad of the silence as she thought about Walter. That's where her mind was when Mrs. Cohen nudged her to tell her they were home.

"It seems it's not only Walter that's smitten." She joked.

As Betty got out of the car Mrs. Cohen reached across the leather seat and pressed a brown paper bag into her hand. Before Betty could say anything she'd pulled the door closed and driven away.

Betty clutched the bag to her breast and ran down the path into the cottage where she lived. She quietly closed the door, knowing at this late hour her father would be in bed. Her mother was waiting up for her as usual. She had the kettle singing on the range, and as she heard the door close behind Betty, she took it from the stand, using a knitted cloth specially made for the job, so that the hot handle didn't burn her hand, and she poured the boiling liquid onto the tea leaves already in the warmed pot. As they waited for the tea to mash Betty showed her mother the bag Mrs. Cohen had given her. She saw a strange look cross her mother's face, just for a second; it was there for so short a time she thought she'd imagined it.

"Open it up then. Don't keep us all in suspense." Her mother tried for levity. But didn't quite make it.

Betty opened the little package. Inside she found two florins, her wages for the last two days and a gold ring, with a silver filigreed ring over the top of the gold one, so that the gold showed through the filigree. The work was so intricate that Betty was afraid to handle it. She dropped it onto the table and stared at it. Her mother picked it up, and Betty could see her mother was quietly crying.

"What is it, Mother? Tell me. What's happened? What's this all about?" She held out the ring in the palm of her hand.

"Sit down Betty and drink your tea."

Betty did as she was bid. Her mother looked questioningly towards the door leading to the stairs, but satisfied her husband hadn't been disturbed, she continued, "It's because I told Mrs. Cohen this morning that you wouldn't be able to help her any more."

"But why, have I done something wrong?" Betty was distraught.

"No, child. It's not anything like that. You've done nothing wrong. Mrs. Burton, you know her. My friend the housekeeper at the Manor?"

Betty nodded. A feeling deep down in her stomach told her what was coming.

"Mrs. Burton and I have known each other for years. Before I married your Dad. Well, she knows you've been looking for a job and ones come up at the Manor. Kitchen maid. She asked me if you'd be interested and I told her yes. It's a good position, Betty." She hurried on, "You'll be working for the cook, Mrs. Thorley. She'll train you up so that one day you'll be a cook."

Betty could see her mother was worried about her reaction. She knew how she loved working with Mrs. Cohen, but Betty also knew that she couldn't do that forever.

She stood up and hugged her mother. "Thanks Mam. When do I have to go?"

"That's just it Betty, it's tomorrow, first thing."

Betty nodded. "I'd better get to bed then."

Her mum nodded.

"I can't take the ring though. It's too much. Will you take it back to Mrs. Cohen and thank her, but explain Mam, when you go to work on Monday?"

"Mr. Cohen made that ages ago just for you. They've been waiting for the proper time to give it to you. When I told her about the job she said she couldn't wait any longer. He had the devil's own job getting your ring size. They'll be really hurt if you give it back. They love you like their own, Betty. You can't give it back."

"But Mam, look at it. It must be worth a fortune."

"They want you to have it. Since I told Mrs. Cohen a couple of weeks ago that this job might come up she's been trying desperately to find some work for you with them, she just hasn't been able to. When you get time off you'll have to go and see her. If you still want to give the ring back you'll have to do it then. Come on finish that tea. We've to be at the Manor for eight."

***

Betty woke at six to the sound of her mother and father talking quietly downstairs in the kitchen.

Her pillow was damp with tears from the previous night. She realised that this was a momentous day in her life. Nothing would ever be the same again for her. She was moving from being a sixteen year old child to being a working woman. She knew she had been lucky. She was an only child; her parents were older than all her friends' parents at school. They had looked like her grandparents when seen with the parents of her peers. She had been born late in the marriage, and her parents had indulged her, feeling so lucky to have her. Most of the girls she'd gone to school with were now working in the laundry or the sewing factories, and had been since leaving school. But she'd never felt pressured to find a job, even though she knew her extra wage would be welcome to her parents. She'd been spoiled, and she knew it.

She loved her parents dearly and although she would have liked to carry on as she had been doing she knew she couldn't. It was not fair on her parents. Her mother had mentioned the job at the Manor coming up some time ago, and she'd never given it another thought; she just hadn't expected it to happen so quickly. Her stomach was doing somersaults as she dressed. She was nervous, she knew everything now was going to change. She would be living away from home. That was her biggest fear. Everything would be so different. She wiped her eyes and dressed. She put on a brave face, not wanting to upset her parents. She knew her father was waiting to see her before he went off to work. He was usually long gone by now. He worked as a woodsman in the forest. The forest was managed by the local council and he worked with others to coppice the place, using Polly, his Shire horse, to drag out the trees felled by the others to a place where they could be loaded onto wagons for transport to the saw mill nearby. Betty wondered when she would next get to visit Polly who was like a pet to her, a great favourite. His wasn't a well-paid job, but as he told people, he was never short of firewood.

She made her way down the stairs and through the batten door, with the black painted sneck handle, at the bottom that led to the kitchen. Her father and mother were sitting together at the kitchen table. Neither spoke. She walked across the room to the Belfast sink situated under the window which looked out onto the shared back yard and washed her face under the icy cold tap which supplied the only water to the little two-up two-down terraced cottage which had been her home for all of her life, and where her parents had spent all their married life.

"What do you want for breakfast?" asked her mother rising from the hard spindle backed chair she'd been sitting on.

"I'm not hungry. A cup of tea will do."

"You should eat something, daughter." Her father always called her that. He liked to say the word, she knew.

"A boiled egg then," she said to please him. She really wasn't hungry at all.

He rose from his chair, identical to the one her mother had used, and crossed the small room to where she was standing in front of the ever glowing fire in the black lead range, where she was warming herself after her wash. He put his arms around her, encompassing her in his total love as well as his strong, weather-beaten arms. He smelled of Polly, Robin cigarettes and pine wood.

He smelled of unconditional love. She held back her tears and clung to him until, gently, he pulled away from her. She could see tears in his eyes also as he said, "I must get off now. Polly will be wondering where I've got too. She'll be wanting her nose-bag."

He kissed her on the top of her head. She hugged him one last time before he left by the back door, and she watched him from the kitchen window as he rode away on his bicycle. She could hear the squeak of his unoiled back wheel long after he'd disappeared from view.

"Do you want the egg, Betty?" her mother asked, pushing a steaming mug of tea across the table to her, now that she'd taken her father's chair. Betty smiled and shook her head, afraid to speak in case her tears should yet fall. Her mother replaced the egg in the bowl from which she'd taken it.

"Drink up then. We've a steady walk in front of us if we're to be there by eight. We don't want you being late on your first day. Do we?"

Betty drank her tea, somewhat reluctantly, as he mother busied herself finishing packing Betty's bag. She watched as she put in her favourite blouse and some stockings. She'd never thought about packing before, but now watching her mother with her case really brought home the enormity of what was happening to her. She was leaving home! She choked back more tears as her mother left the room swiftly. Betty knew she was going out to dry her eyes too.

Betty put her unfinished mug under the tap and rinsed it out before upturning it on the, scrubbed wooden draining board by the big, stone sink. She put on her gabardine coat and checked, woollen headscarf, which matched the one her mother was wearing and then had one last look around the kitchen she'd known for so long before the two of them set off on the three mile walk to the Manor.

Soon they were out of the village and into the pleasant country lanes which surrounded it, and which would eventually lead to their destination. The trees were just starting to shed their leaves, and because of the lack of wind were beautifully coloured in reds, yellows and browns. Here and there some of the hardier ones were still almost full green. The weather was still unseasonably warm giving the farmers ample time to bring in their crops. The fields alongside the road they were taking were filled with sheaves of corn, stooked to allow the wind to blow through and dry it.

Awaiting the men with their pitchforks and horse drawn wagons to come and load it up before taking it to the barns to store it against the winter that would surely come.

After just over an hour's walk they reached the low wall which grew in height as they walked beside it, until it reached a height of eight feet, where it formed great pillars with heraldic beasts in stone atop. The stone beasts were now unrecognizable, wind blasted and weathered as they were. They guarded a gravel drive leading up to a house which couldn't be seen from the lane where they now stood. Although the large wrought iron gates, painted black and gold, stood invitingly open Betty's mother continued to walk on for another twenty minutes or so, following the red brick wall as it began again to reduce in height, until they reached a much less imposing wooden gate, overhung by a brick arch, sprung from pillars built into the now four feet high wall. Behind the wooden gate, which squeaked as they opened it to pass through, reminding her of her father's bicycle, and causing her eyes to sting, she wiped them surreptitiously they stepped onto a York stone path. They followed the path which led to the rear of the Manor House, where upon knocking at the large, black painted, studded oak door they were greeted by Mrs Burton.

Betty was terrified. If it hadn't been for the calming presence of her mother she would surely have run away.

Mrs. Burton shook hands with Betty's mother and then with Betty herself. After the introductions she led them into a passage, arched over and white painted, along which as they walked, Betty noticed a number of doors leading off. At the end of this passage was Mrs Burton's private sitting room, which they entered. Inside a table had been prepared with cups and saucers. A pot of tea stood upon it under a woollen tea cosy.

"I like to start the day with a nice cup of tea. Don't you? You'll both be ready for one, I suppose, after your walk. I'm sure." She ushered them into brightly coloured, easy chairs, with white antimacassars on the backs. The chairs faced a blazing coal fire, freshly stoked. She proceeded to pour. "Milk? Sugar?"

Betty declined the sugar in honour of Mrs. Cohen.

Over the next half hour Mrs. Burton did her best to put Betty at her ease. She knew as her mother and Mrs. Burton chatted that not every girl coming to work at the Manor was treated to a cup of tea in the house-keepers apartments. She felt privileged, but there was still trepidation there. Betty was frightened of what was to come. The fear of the unknown. She drank her tea quietly, balancing the dainty cup and saucer carefully on her knee. Terrified of dropping it. It was a far cry from her own white mug sitting on the draining board at home. Her eyes prickled again. She took a deep breath and listened to her mother and her friend talk about things she knew nothing of. After a while there was a knock at the door. Mrs. Burton opened it to a small, white-faced girl, in the brown shift dress and white pinafore and hat that was the uniform of the house.

"Oh! Is it that time already?" Mrs. Burton checked the small gold watch on her fleshy wrist. "This is Jenny. She's come to take you, Betty, and show you to your room. You'll be sharing with Jenny. She's a nice girl." As she said this she looked at Betty's mother and nodded conspiratorially.

Mrs. Burton stood aside as Betty and her mum hugged in front of the now roaring fire.

"Goodbye, Betty, I'll see you in a couple of weeks' time." Betty's mum kissed her and turned to the fire.

Betty followed Mrs. Burton to the door and thanked her for the tea. As she stepped out into the corridor, fighting back tears, unsuccessfully, she was introduced formally to Jenny. Jenny curtsied as Mrs Burton introduced them and then she said, "Go with Jenny now Betty. She knows where you're going to be working. I'll go back now and say goodbye to your mother. I'm sure you'll settle right in." As she said this she laid a calming hand on Betty's shoulder. Jenny stood at the end of the corridor and waited, pretending not to see Betty's tears.

Mrs. Burton stepped back into her sitting room and closed the door. To Betty it felt like a door closing on her former life. She sobbed. "This way duck." Jenny smiled a wan smile, "I felt just the same when I came. First time away from home is it?"

Betty could only nod, afraid of breaking down completely in front of her new companion.

"We'll have a minute when we get up to the room. No one expects much out of you today. It'll be different tomorrow mind. But they're good here. You're lucky to get a place here. These places are well sort after. Everyone around here in service talks about working here. I thank my lucky stars every day, I do. The last place I was before this, well, I shudder to think..." Jenny's voice trailed off.

Her face showed what she was thinking, and this gave Betty time to compose herself. They were climbing a spiral, stone staircase, one side of which, as they climbed, Betty noticed felt warm. Jenny noticed her touching the wall as they climbed.

"That's the kitchen flue behind there. The fire's never let out in the kitchen, so that flue, and our rooms, are always warm. "She opened a white painted wooden door with a black sneck. "Here we are... No matter how cold it gets in winter. She grinned, and stood back on the threshold to let Betty enter.

The room was small and contained two single beds with a large dark brown stained, double wardrobe standing between them. There was a small table standing in front of the garret window and on this stood a large water jug in a bowl. Betty noticed small red flowers around the spout and the edge of the bowl. Above what turned out to be Jenny's bed, was a religious picture of a kind Betty had never seen before. It was the only decoration in the all-white, spotlessly clean room. Jenny noticed Betty looking. "It's the Sacred Heart. My mum's Irish and a catholic. She gave it to me, says it'll look after me. I prayed to it at my last job. Asked it to get me away. I ended up here, so now I hang it over my bed." She ended a little lamely.

Betty smiled and sat on her bed wishing she had a Sacred Heart to pray to. Jenny sat opposite her on her own bed and reached across, taking Betty's hand in her own. "It's not as bad as you're thinking. Honest it isn't. It's hard work, but it's fun. Once you've got to know everyone you'll enjoy it. You mark my words, girl." She squeezed Betty's hand and looked deep into her eyes. Betty cried again and Jenny sat and held her hand until she was finished. "That's it now. No more tears. Listen to me talk! I cried for two days when I first left home. But that was at a much worse place than this. So no more now, eh? We don't want 'em all to see you like this do we?" Betty shook her head, feeling really stupid. She leaned across to hug Jenny and thank her for her patience, in doing so she kicked something under her own bed with her heel.

"That's the guzzunda, as my Dad calls it. If you use it you have to carry it all the way downstairs to empty it. I try never to use mine." Jenny said seriously.

Betty didn't know what to say, and after a second or two both girls were laid back on their respective beds in fits of laughter. When finally the laughter had subsided Betty queried, "Guzzunda?"

Jenny looked at her quizzically for a moment, "It guzzunda the bed doesn't it?"

This required more laughter and rolling about on the beds. Betty realised that there was more than a little hysteria in her laughter but she felt better for it and after this episode she felt much more relaxed about her situation. While this atmosphere prevailed Jenny sensibly got Betty into her uniform ill -fitting though it was. The fitting brought on more laughter and the tears were not tears of sorrow now, as Jenny tried to get the little white hat to balance on Betty's unruly, curly, black hair. Finally Betty was ready.

While Betty and Jenny were rolling about on their beds, Betty's mother had said goodbye to Mrs. Burton and was making her way down the Yorkstone path to the arched gate on her way home. At the wooden, squeaky gate she turned and looked back at the large, imposing, red brick building, wondering where Betty was at that moment and questioning whether she'd done the right thing in leaving her there. After reflecting for some little time she opened the gate and passed through beginning her long trudge home alone, full of misgivings. Had she seen Betty at that moment it would have saved her a fortnight of sleepless nights, wondering if she'd done the right thing.

But such are the travails of parenthood.

CHAPTER THREE.

Betty meanwhile, dressed and be-capped was presented to Mrs. Thorley, the cook. Betty had washed her face and although her eyes were red rimmed, Jenny assured her that you couldn't tell she had been crying. But only Betty believed her.

Mrs. Thorley was a small woman. Slightly stooped and with a shock of dark curly hair, which she kept under her mob cap with difficulty. Invariably over the course of the day it fought its way out innumerable times, and had to be pushed back under, where it began its fight for freedom all over again, immediately. This left Mrs. Thorley, depending, of course on what she was doing, with streaks of flour across her forehead and in her hair. Woe betide anyone who dared to mention it to her! She was authoritative and didn't suffer fools gladly, but she was a kind person and behind her bluff exterior she really cared about the people who worked under her, provided they showed willing. She had no time for slackers. Jenny had explained this to Betty on their way down the stairs and now Betty was quite looking forward to meeting Mrs. Thorley. Betty wasn't afraid of hard work, so as long as what Jenny had said was true, she was sure she would get on with the cook. And so it proved. There was an instant rapport between them and Betty felt comfortable in the cook's company. Which was fortunate because Jenny was sent away as soon as the introductions were over to get back to her own duties.

Mrs. Thorley, whose name was Audrey, but it was months before Betty could bring herself to be so informal with the cook, told Betty what her duties would be. She was to help Mrs. Thorley, Audrey, by preparing vegetables, which the gardeners would bring from the gardens and leave on the table outside the kitchen door. Mrs. Thorley took Betty across the large, white-tiled, room to an oversized door in the right-hand corner of the room and opened it.

Outside was a yard, bigger than the combined yards outside her mother and father's cottage. Opposite the kitchen door was a single storey building with a lean-to type slate roof. This building had two rough sawn, batten doors with sneck latches on the front of it. The left-hand door was the fuel store. Both logs and coal were stored there. The right-hand door was where Betty would learn to prepare meat brought to them by the farm hands and the gardeners. Sometimes there would be game from the gamekeepers. To the right of the door there was a long wooden trestle table which was laden with fruit and vegetables. "Your job for today Betty," said the cook, "is to clean and prepare those." She pointed to the table groaning under the weight of the produce on it.

Betty thought, but didn't say anything, that there was enough on the table to feed an army.

"What we need first," she leaned behind her and took a clip-board from a nail knocked into a board fixed to the wall above a large, low, deep sink, "will be these things from this list. Every day I'll make up a list like this. You prepare the vegetables from this list first. These will be used over the length of the day according to a menu I've arranged with the Major or his wife. The amounts will vary depending on whether, or how many guests there are. The Major entertains a lot." She nodded sagely.

I can see, thought Betty looking at the groaning table.

"I've already prepared the meat and by the smell of it, it needs basting. So you start with the carrots and potatoes.

33

Weigh them on those old scales there." She pointed to a pair of scales under an open-fronted lean-to at the end of the table. "The amounts are written alongside each item on the list. Wash them in the bucket sink, and then finish them off in the Belfast sink next to it. Once they're prepared leave them on the draining board and I'll get them from there as I need them. OK?" With that she was off to the oven on the opposite wall to the door, where she took out a large pork joint, which smelled delicious to a girl who hadn't had any breakfast, and she started to spoon the liquor from the roasting tin over the already browning, scored skin.

Betty looked at her list, two pounds of carrots, six pounds of potatoes two cauliflowers, six parsnips and two savoy cabbages. Must have guests, she thought.

Betty began her first day at work proper; she didn't count the walk, the tea with Mrs. Burton, or the emotional time with Jenny, or even getting into the uniform, this, for her was where the work began. Doing the job. She worked out that the low, deep sink was the bucket sink, and it was in here that the preliminary washing took place. The heaviest dirt was removed in the freezing cold water running from the large brass tap. The vegetables weren't too dirty as the weather had been reasonably dry. Betty thought that it would be a different job in the winter when the produce was heavy with mud. The cold water from the tap would be colder then, and today her hands were already blue. She could see that the gardener had rinsed the greens already, some of them were still dripping wet, it was a help. She hoped he continued to do it when there was ice on the vegetables.

After removal of the heaviest dirt, the veg was washed again in the Belfast sink and, using a knife which hung above the sink on a hempen line, she took off the leaves from the root vegetables. Then using a paring knife she peeled them and placed them on the wooden draining board as instructed.

Mrs. Thorley had disappeared so she looked around the large kitchen for somewhere to put the peelings and leaves. Under the draining board she found two, deep white enamel buckets, she decided these must be for the waste, as she could find nothing else. She put the peelings in them.

Having now cleaned and peeled the carrots and potatoes, she looked for the next thing on her list. Two cauliflowers, two savoy cabbages and six parsnips. Back she went to the table. She quickly found the cauliflowers and the parsnips but could only find one savoy cabbage. She took in what she had and got to work. She was just finishing the last parsnip when Mrs. Thorley re-appeared. She came over to the drainer as Betty began to strip the outer leaves from the lone savoy. "There's only one savoy, Mrs. Thorley." She informed her, pointing at it as she worked.

Mrs. Thorley was looking through everything Betty had done. Turning over the items in her hand and replacing them on the board after inspection. "You've been busy Betty, Where are the peelings?" she looked quizzically around the room.

"I didn't know where to put them so I used those buckets from under the drainer." Betty pointed, with trepidation, worried now that she'd done something wrong.

"Very good, very good," grinned the cook, showing crooked teeth. They're the floor buckets that the stove girl uses to mop the floor but they're as good as anything for now. One savoy you say." She picked up the buckets containing the peelings and said, "Follow me."

She walked to the door leading out to the yard, putting one bucket down to open it. Betty picked up this bucket, the cook nodded and led the way outside. She pointed to a large galvanised bucket that was battered and rusty. It had obviously seen better days. It stood against the wall of the outbuilding with the two doors. "We use that for the peelings normally." She led Betty across the front of the outbuilding to two large, round, galvanised bins like tall dustbins, by the corner.

"This one is where we put the peelings." The bin was marked with a white painted cross. "That one," she pointed to the unmarked one, "is for any offal we don't use, feathers, skin's and bones that sort of waste. The man from the rendering plant calls once or twice a week and empties that one. The other, the one with the cross goes down to the pig sties. They make it into pig swill. On a bad day when the wind's in the wrong direction you can smell them cooking it up. The blacksmith on the farm made the bins. They take them down the path," she pointed to a path alongside the garden wall which obviously joined the path Betty had walked earlier in the day with her mother, "to the lane where they empty them onto a trailer. The renderer has his own wagon."

"They use all of it?" Betty wrinkled up her nose while emptying her bucket into the marked bin.

"Mostly. Yes. I don't think they'll sort through it. Do you? I think anything left over is composted."

They both laughed.

"Has your dad got an allotment?"

Betty wondered at the change of subject, as they carried the empty buckets across the yard, and back into the kitchen. "Yes. He grows all sorts, all our veg comes from his garden. He grows soft fruits as well. It helps out a lot. He doesn't earn a big wage."

"I thought so; the last girl who had your job couldn't tell a parsnip from a pineapple."

They both laughed as they closed the big door behind them.

"You'd better rinse out Dora's buckets or she'll have something to say. I wonder why they only brought up one savoy. I'm sure I asked for two." She went back outside to the still loaded table to check.

When she came back in she shrugged her shoulders, "We've enough for the master anyway. We'll have to make do with what's left." She must have noticed Betty's look. As she went on to clarify. "We cook for the staff as well. We have what the Major eats, I just cook extra. We all eat here. The live-in staff that is." She pointed to the large, well-scrubbed, table which dominated the centre of the room. "And if we don't get a move on the meal will be late. Get that chopping board and start on the potatoes, cut 'em like this," she quartered one. "Keep all the pieces, roughly the same size and they'll not go mushy."

Betty did as she was told and soon the veg all was bubbling away nicely on the stove. Dora came in just as the last pan was going on and Mrs. Thorley nodded towards the newly washed buckets under the draining board. They both grinned knowingly at each other.

"Kettle's going on Dora. You ready for a sandwich Betty?" asked the cook, knowing the answer already.

"I am," said Dora before Betty had time to answer.

That was Betty's introduction to Dora.

They all looked at one another and laughed. "Make the tea Betty," said Audrey, pointing to a large brown tea pot standing near the range. The kettle was already singing when Dora came in from the yard with a bucket of coal. Betty took the coal from her, while she went back for logs. While this was going on Audrey cut slices from a loaf of bread and some slices from the chicken left over from yesterday's dinner for the sandwiches. Soon, the fire freshly stoked, the three of them sat down to their meal, with steaming mugs of tea. As they ate Betty thought back to Jenny's words, only a tearful, short couple of hours ago, "They're all right when you get to know them." Betty smiled to herself. I'm going to be all right, she thought, and took a big bite out of her delicious sandwich.

***

The day went by rapidly after lunch. Various other members of staff drifted in for tea and sandwiches. Betty was introduced to them by Audrey, and was kept busy supplying the food and drink. By the time Jenny appeared Betty was in sole charge of lunch, as Audrey was busy making marmalade. The Major liked it with his breakfast, Audrey confided. Jenny's was a flying visit, as she was preparing the dining room for dinner. Betty thought her new friend had really just popped in to see how she was getting on, and Betty realised what a good group of people she'd been lucky enough to join, and to be able work with.

Soon it was time to plate up the dishes to be carried upstairs by the dumb waiter where the staff, Jenny among them, would serve dinner. In the kitchen Betty laid the large table for six. There was to be Lily, the upstairs maid. She was engaged to the grocer's son in the village so Dora had informed her. Then there was Albert, the butler. He was red-faced, tall man, rather portly, who said he was sixty, but everyone thought he was older. Dora said it was the port that made him red faced and portly. Audrey shushed her, but had laughed when she made the remark at lunchtime. Dora, Jenny, Audrey, and herself made up the staff who lived in and who would be at dinner as soon as the dumb waiter delivered the empty dinner service to be washed. There were other staff but they lived on, or around the estate. Just by the garden there stood a row of cottages where the gardeners and some of the farm staff lived.

"You'll see them soon enough," Dora had said at dinner.

Audrey, who Betty still thought of as Mrs. Thorley, said, not entirely joking, that Dora was the font of all knowledge at the Manor. Betty found out later in her time there that Dora was the longest serving member of staff, and, although it was never mentioned, she was said to be older than the portly Albert.

So it was that Betty's first day at the Manor drew to a close, after helping to do the dishes and put them away. At nine o'clock that night, after fifteen hours, which started so traumatically and ended so enjoyably, she followed Jenny up the winding stairs to bed. Once in the room she flopped down on to her bed and had it not been for Jenny prodding her she would have been asleep in seconds.

"Hang up your uniform, Betty. If it's creased you'll be in trouble. The Major's a stickler about neatness."

Betty dragged herself to her feet and did as she was bid. Soon she was wrapped up in her woollen blankets listening to Jenny talking about one of the farm boys who'd asked her out. She never heard which one it was because by the light of the moon through the window (neither of them felt the need to draw the curtains) she was asleep. Just as she dozed off, as she was trying and failing to listen to Jenny's story, she remembered she'd promised to see Walter that night at the fair, but it was too late, she was asleep and Walter was just a dream.

***

Three miles away, it was a different story. Her mother tossed and turned in her bed worrying if she had done the right thing, and was Betty all right. By her side her father feigned sleep but his thoughts ran along the same lines.

***

That evening at the Goose Fair, Mrs. Cohen noticed Walter hanging around the coconut shy for most of the night, but being on her own, watching both stalls, she had no time to call him over and explain what had happened. Eventually, as the fair drew to a close, she caught sight of him, head down, disconsolately kicking a stone along the ground as he walked off, hands in his pockets and alone, his friends having long since left him and gone home. She called to him then, but it was too late and he never heard her. Soon he was lost to her sight, as she, also alone, began to tidy up the stalls.

CHAPTER FOUR.

The next day began with a wash in the basin under the window and a breakfast of bacon and eggs in the kitchen with Dora, Jenny and Audrey. It was five thirty a.m. After the meal the other two went to their respective jobs leaving Audrey, now Mrs. Thorley again, with Betty. "We didn't manage to clear the vegetable table yesterday Betty. Just check now and see what's left, will you dear!"

Betty remembered the creaking table full, but when she looked there were only a few beetroots and a few carrots left.

"They've all but gone, Mrs. Thorley. Someone must have been in the night." Betty was a little uncertain of what to do. She'd never been in a position where something had been stolen before.

"Bring in and clean what's left Betty. They'll be bringing more presently." Mrs. Thorley didn't seem at all put out by the theft. "And it's Audrey."

"What are we to do about the missing veg?" Betty asked. A little put out by Mrs. Thorley's attitude to the loss.

"Oh! It'll be the lads that's taken 'em."

"The lads?"

"Oh aye! The Major lets the lads, anyone who works here as a matter of fact, take any veg they want from the table at evening time. There's plenty to go round. That's why the lads bring so much up. Then, like today we use up what's left. Or store it if we can. We'll pickle the beetroot and use the carrots for dinner."

"I thought they'd been stolen in the night," she said relieved.

Mrs. Thorley grinned. "You weren't to know."

Betty cleaned and prepared as before, checking her list as she went along. While they worked they talked. Betty learned that Mrs. Burton's husband was the estate manager, but in actual fact he mainly looked after the Major's horses. The Major was a great horse lover and rode nearly every day with Mr. Burton. They were more friends than employee and employer. That was the Major's style, Mrs. Thorley said. The Burtons ate with the Major and his wife every night, unless there was a really big dinner or some such occasion on. At those times they ate in their private rooms. That wasn't to say they put themselves above the rest of the staff. They didn't by any means. The Burton's were very like the Major and his wife, it was just that the housekeeper liked the staff to be able to talk freely amongst themselves and she felt sometimes her presence stopped them doing that. If Betty had any problems at all Mrs. Thorley advised her to go to Mrs. Burton who, she assured her, would listen to her, and would sort out anything troubling her. Mrs. Burton was a lovely woman. Betty was pleased to hear it, especially as she'd got her chance at the Manor through her mother's friendship with her.

When the beetroot was boiling nicely on the range, Mrs. Thorley – "Audrey, please," – took Betty to the cold cellars, where extra veg was stored for the winter months, particularly root crops. So now when Betty was told to prepare stuff for storage, she knew where it went.

Next stop was the meat shed. This was the place Betty had been dreading. She'd seen her mother cleaning rabbits or game birds that her father had brought home from the forest and she'd thought as she'd watched, that she never wanted to have to do that.

The shed was cold. It had one window which covered half the wall opposite to the door. The door was on the low side of the lean-to. There were open wooden beams supporting the pan-tiled roof. Into these beams hooks had been driven and a brace of pheasants hung from one of them. Mrs. Thorley expertly poked at them and shook her head. "Not ready yet. You have to wait for the meat to drop, about a fortnight usually. When it's warm though it could be quicker. You've got to keep your eye on them."

Betty looked around the small room. Below the window was a wooden bench, well-scrubbed. Into the bench two large nails had been hammered. These stuck up about four inches from the bed of the bench. The floor was made of brick and was also scrubbed clean. There was a cupboard on the wall to the left of the bench, but other than that the place was empty. Betty was relieved. She didn't know what she had expected but she was for the moment, pleasantly surprised. She didn't like the place though, and she shivered.

"In here," Mrs. Thorley opened the cupboard, "are the knives you'll need." Inside hung a row of gleaming butcher's knives. "When the time comes I'll show you what to do. Nobody likes this job, not if you've owt about you. But if you're cook it's a job that's got to be done, and if you do it yourself you know it's been done right. That's what I say. We only do the game in here. Skinning and such. The other beasts are slaughtered elsewhere. We dress the meat in here though. You'll come in here and there'll likely be a side of beef or half a pig hanging when it's time. We'll need to do them together when the time comes. Just so you know, Betty."

Betty nodded, dreading the day.

"Anyway, let's get out of here. It's time for Dora's tea, and we might as well have one ourselves." Mrs. Thorley tried to lighten the mood.

They left the building and Betty happily closed the door; she followed Mrs. Thorley into the kitchen thinking, there was one part of being a cook she wasn't going to like.

Dora was already there and as Betty closed the kitchen door, shivering from the cold of the meat shed and welcoming the warmth of the kitchen, Jenny entered by the house door opposite. Mrs. Thorley was pouring steaming water onto the tea leaves in the big brown pot, as Betty pulled out one of the heavy wooden chairs and she and Jenny sat down together at the table. Mrs. Thorley poured the tea into the large, white mugs through the tea strainer; no cups in the kitchen. Everyone was ready for this drink. As Betty picked up her steaming mug they heard a noise outside. Betty rose and opened the yard door, to find the cause of the sound was a small boy in an oversized coat and hat, depositing vegetables on the table. He was very thin and doffed his cap in a familiar way, which made Betty smile.

"Is that the veg arriving, Betty?" asked Mrs. Thorley.

"Some of it," answered Betty. "Mostly greens."

"Get your tea, we've plenty of time."

Jenny nodded and grinned across as Betty sat down again. "Who delivered the veg?" she asked as nonchalantly as possible.

"Not who you think," butted in Dora, cackling.

"Jenny blushed. "I didn't think it was anyone," she blustered.

"Why did you ask then?" persevered Dora.

"It was a small thin lad in a big coat and hat," interjected Betty, seeing Jenny blushing and at a loss.

"Not the right one then." Dora cackled mischievously and slurped her tea.

Mrs. Thorley shook her head at the two of them. "Take no notice of her," she nodded towards Dora who cackled again into her mug. "You didn't ought to say anything to her you know. I have told you before."

Dora laughed again as Jenny looked shamefaced and drank her tea quickly before hurrying off.

"You shouldn't tease her so." Mrs. Thorley scolded Dora gently.

"I know. But I can't help it. She's so easy. "They both laughed. Betty kept quiet, worrying about her friend.

When Dora left and they were busy at their respective jobs Mrs. Thorley noticed how quiet Betty was and said, "Don't worry about Jenny and Dora, Betty; they've been like that since Jenny came. Dora loves to needle people and Jenny's always giving her ammunition. But they both know there's no harm in it. In fact Dora thinks the world of Jenny."

Betty nodded and scrubbed harder at the swede she was cleaning. "What was that about then?"

"One of the farm hands asked Jenny out and she made the mistake of telling Dora. Now Dora's desperately trying to find out which lad it is, and Jenny won't tell."

"She mentioned something about a lad to me last night."

"That's just what I mean, not that you'd tease her, but she can't keep anything to herself. That lad who brought the veg he was the youngest lad of the head gardener. It certainly wasn't going to be him sparking our Jenny."

"Sparking?" Betty laughed.

"You never heard that before? You'll hear a lot more than that, girl. I can vouch." Mrs. Thorley pounded at the dough she was kneading for the bread, smiling. She made bread twice a week: Mondays and Thursdays.

The day continued much as Sunday had. Betty and Mrs. Thorley chatted amicably throughout the day, and Betty felt comfortable in Mrs. Thorley's company, as if she'd known her all her life. Although try as she may she couldn't call her Audrey. It had been the same with Mrs. Cohen, Naomi.

She had the same companionable friendship with her but still felt uncomfortable calling her Naomi. For a moment Betty's thought's drifted to the fair and to the good times she'd had there, but then she heard Mrs. Thorley's voice and realised she was still talking about the gardener's sons.

She revealed that he had three sons. The one she'd seen was David; he was the youngest. Then there were Albert and Walter. All three of them worked for the Major.

Albert, the oldest, was the pig-man; he came and took away the kitchen waste for the swill. He had a big boiler down by the sties, made for him by the blacksmith, where he boiled the swill up. On days when the wind was in the right direction, you could smell it as she'd already mentioned, but Betty didn't correct her. She wrinkled up her flour-dusted nose.

Then there was Walter. He looked after the birds. There were ducks, chicken, geese and he had doves. When he wasn't looking after them he helped his dad around the garden. It would probably be Walter who brought up the eggs.

When Mrs. Thorley mentioned Walter, she thought of her Walter at the fair and the arrangements she'd made and not been able to keep. She almost told Mrs. Thorley what had happened; in this atmosphere of camaraderie she could see how Jenny could be inveigled into telling secrets to Dora. But mindful of what she'd been told, she held her counsel. She would go and see Mrs. Cohen when she got her time off and just see if Walter showed up, and if he came to the shy and said anything. Here she was spending all this time thinking about him and, maybe, he didn't show up himself. He was painfully shy. She felt herself grinning, thinking of their meeting; she was confident he would have shown up, but it seemed so long ago now. Mrs. Thorley had been watching Betty, as these thoughts ran through her mind and showed, graphically, on her face. She asked astutely, "Have you got a young man Betty?"

"Why no, Mrs. Thorley. I have not," she replied, perhaps a little too vehemently.

"Only asked."

Mrs. Thorley grinned.

Betty blushed, to the roots of her hair.

Mrs. Thorley grinned more widely.

The day closed with Jenny showing Betty the staff bathroom. It was one of the doors off the long white entrance corridor. Jenny explained that the staff had use of the bathroom whenever they wanted in their own time, but it must be kept clean. Betty had never seen anything like it: a proper fitted bath with both hot and cold running water which came out of taps. Her bath at home had been a tin one in front of the fire on a Sunday night. When not in use the bath would hang from a nail knocked into the brickwork of the outside chemical toilet at the bottom of the backyard.

"Can I have a bath now?" Betty asked, visualising herself in the tub.

"You don't have to ask my permission. If you want a bath now girl, get one. Have you soap and stuff?"

"Upstairs in my bag."

"You draw your bath, I'll get it for you. I'm getting mine anyway."

So Betty, for the first time in her life, climbed into a real porcelain bath. Luxury.

That night she and Jenny, both scrubbed clean as new pins, lay in bed and as usual Jenny talked. Betty relaxed and listened, as she drifted off to sleep dreaming of steaming, hot water running from gold taps. Jenny still talking about her young man, Betty luxuriated in the steaming foam. Disconcertingly for Betty, just as she was drifting into sleep, Walter turned off the water to her bath.

CHAPTER FIVE.

The next ten days flew by for Betty. She now regularly met David as he brought up the vegetables to the table.

They even began to pass a few words. But David was very shy and the words passed were cursory. Mrs. Thorley was subtly getting Betty doing some cooking. Almost without her noticing, she was kneading bread and checking it as it baked. She began to understand cooking times, and she would check pans when Mrs. Thorley wasn't around, which as part of her teaching method, was quite often.

Betty was also beginning to understand the eccentricities of the range. It's hot and cold spots. Where to stand baking trays in the oven to get the best results, and which pans to use for what.

The weekend crept up on Betty in a blur of oven heat and steam. "Day off tomorrow Betty. What've you got planned?" asked Mrs. Thorley at tea break.

Betty looked blankly at her. She hadn't thought about time off. "I don't know. I'll go and see Mam and Dad I suppose."

Mrs. Thorley grinned certain now that Betty had settled in. She had been unsure at first about whether or not Betty could settle down away from home. She seemed such a home bird in the first few days. Some girls just weren't cut out for this type of work. But now she was sure Betty would make it.

"Mrs. Burton told me she was going into the village in the morning if you wanted a lift. She's taking the trap."

"That would be lovely."

"She'll be at the gate at seven thirty. Don't be late or you'll be walking. She doesn't hang about."

The following morning, Sunday, dawned bright and cold. Betty was at the gate early, wrapped in a scarf her mother had knitted for her, and was surprised to see a man she didn't know, driving the little brown and grey mare, pulling Mrs. Burton's trap along the lane.

"Perfect timing." Mrs. Burton spoke from behind Betty, making her jump. She must have followed her down the path and Betty hadn't heard her.

The man driving the trap laughed, "She's like a cat, my missus."

Mrs. Burton slapped him on the shoulder as he dismounted and handed her the reins.

"You'll be Betty." He held out a strong, calloused, weather-browned hand, which Betty shook as she curtsied. "I'm John Burton."

"Pleased to meet you, sir."

"No need for all that. Enjoy your day off. My regards to your parents." He kissed Mrs. Burton on the cheek and was gone.

"Jump in Betty. I bet you can't wait to see your mum and dad?"

"No. You're right." Betty was beginning to feel the excitement now as they sped through the lanes to the clip clopping of the little mare's hooves. She was still a little in awe of Mrs. Burton and wasn't quite sure what to say.

"I'm only going to be in the village for an hour, Betty so you'll have to walk back." Mrs. Burton apologised.

"It's very kind of you to take me in, Mrs. Burton. Thank you."

Mrs. Burton just shook her head. "I'm going in anyway, it's no trouble. I'll drop you at the corner. Is that all right?"

"Perfect." That was right at the end of her street. She was sure Mrs. Burton had got the trap out just to take her home on her first day off. Which was what she told her mother at the tearful reunion ten minutes later.

Her mother had laid the table so they could have breakfast, she'd expected to see her father there, but he'd had to go to work. He'd be home for lunch her mother said. Wild horses wouldn't keep him away. She laughed, relieved now her daughter was home and appeared to be enjoying her job. Maybe now she'd get a full night's sleep.

After breakfast they went to see Mrs. Cohen. Another tearful reunion; it was as if she'd been away months. It slowly dawned on her how much these people loved her and how much she loved them in return.

As they walked home everyone she passed asked how she was getting on; it seemed the whole village knew she'd gone to work at the Manor.

Lunchtime and her father was home. A more restrained reunion this time, but no less loving for that. The tears were all hers, well nearly all. The ones she could see!

He asked her how she was doing and if she liked the work. Now they were both together she could tell them everything she'd been learning. She could see her enthusiasm put them both at their ease, especially her mother. Over the rabbit pie, especially made as it was her favourite, she told them everything that had happened to her over the last two weeks ending with the bath with the gold taps [polished brass really, but she didn't tell them that] and hot and cold running water.

Her parents sat and listened as she talked. They were both proud of her, but both of them felt a little sad, as they admitted to each other later that evening, when they'd walked her back to the Manor, in the dusk. Returning home in the dark, they held hands as they walked, just as they had in their youth. The scents of late autumn filled their nostrils and the sounds of the countryside going to bed or the rustlings of the nocturnal predators waking up accompanied them on their bittersweet journey home. As darkness fell and the stars filled the clear, frosty, sky they talked quietly about their beloved daughter. Memories of her early childhood filled their conversation. Both of them could now feel her slipping away. She was growing up. They both realised that for the last sixteen years they'd been pleased she'd been such a home bird. That she hadn't wanted to leave and get a job as many of her school friends had. Mrs. Cohen had been an unwitting ally in this, with her coconut shy, and allowing her to help her mother out with the cleaning. But now she was gone and although they were pleased it was a sad time for them both, especially her mother. The house was quiet now, all the time. Even at Mrs. Cohen's when she was at work and when Mrs. Cohen was at Mr. Cohen's workshop with her husband, her house was as silent as the grave; whereas normally she would have heard Betty's incessant chatter now there was only silence. Her husband had his workmates to talk to, and Polly to look after, so she felt Betty's departure the most. There were a few tears as they opened the gate and entered the quiet cottage. They hugged each other behind the closed door in the dark as they realised it was a rite of passage for them as much as it was for Betty. He stoked the fire to boil the kettle for a nightcap before bed, while she readied the pot. They didn't light the gas mantle but used the light from the fire only, as they drank the warming tea, both surrounded by their own particular memories of Betty, before going silently to bed.

Betty on the other hand found Jenny and Mrs. Thorley still in the kitchen and over her night-time cup of tea, in between telling her friends about her day off, she heard all the gossip of the day at the Manor. Finally, her first day off was completed to perfection with a steaming soak in the bath before curling up in bed and listening to Jenny talking about her young man as she drifted off into a dreamless sleep.

The following day, fully refreshed, she was first into the kitchen. She brought in the vegetables left from the day before and had them cleaned and stored before Mrs. Thorley made an appearance. She had been discussing some household matters with Mrs. Burton, she explained. "Has that boy been with the eggs yet?" she queried.

Betty opened the door to look. "He's coming up the path now," she called over her shoulder from the threshold.

"He's become very tardy lately that one. Not at all like David. I'll have to have a word with his father."

Betty could say nothing. She gave an involuntary grunt and stepped back into the kitchen.

"Whatever's the matter Betty? You look as if you've seen a ghost."

"It's nothing Mrs. Thorley."

"Is he here yet? I need those eggs."

Betty stepped out into the yard and went over to the table as the boy carrying the trug containing the eggs put them down. "Walter?"

He jumped back from the table as if he'd been shot and looked up. All the way up from the garden he'd been kicking a stone in front of him. Not looking, or caring where he was going. Now *he* looked as if he'd seen a ghost. "Betty? Betty, what are you doing here?"

"Is he here yet, Betty? He used to be the best of them. What has happened to him? I bet it's a girl and I know nowt," shouted Mrs. Thorley through the open door.

"I'll have to take these in. Wait a minute."

Walter nodded. Uncertain, astonished, his head in a spin, but completely happy. Certainly happy. She remembered him. And moreover, she wanted to talk to him. What about though? Doubt began to set in, to cloud his mind. That thought tempered his euphoria as she came back out of the kitchen and into the yard.

"I've only got a minute."

He nodded unable to speak now she was here, standing in front of him.

She herself didn't know what to say now the time had come. They stood looking at each other.

"What are you doing here?" he finally asked.

"I work here. That's why I couldn't meet you at the fair. I didn't know, but my Mam had fixed me up with a job here. I started on the day I was supposed to meet you." It came out so quickly, she hoped it wasn't garbled. It sounded garbled in her head; spoken too quickly in order to get it all out. She looked into his eyes hoping he'd understood.

He just stood looking at her. Unable to take in what, she'd just said.

"I'll have to go." She turned on her heel and headed back into the kitchen.

"I'll bring some more stuff up later." He called as she entered the door almost knocking Mrs. Thorley over as she did so.

"So that's what's been up with him is it?" she said knowingly.

Betty blushed to the roots of her hair.

"We wondered what had happened to him. He was always such a good lad. You could do worse, lass." She nodded knowingly.

"It's not... " Betty's sentence trailed off.

"We all said that. Aye, and meant it no doubt. Get on with those carrots while I cook breakfast. You can tell me all about it then."

Mrs. Thorley busied herself with the bacon and eggs while Betty tried to concentrate on what she was doing. The coincidence astonished her! She had never for one moment thought that the Walter mentioned by Mrs. Thorley could have been the Walter she'd arranged to meet at the fair. Walter was such a common name, it had never crossed her mind.

"Tea up." It was Dora. She must have smelled the bacon cooking.

Betty's heart was in her mouth as she sat down at the table. Then the door opened and in walked Jenny. Now, she thought, once this got out, she'd be the talk of the house, what would Walter think!

She sat, head down, over her meal. "Cut the bread Betty," smiled Mrs. Thorley, "What's got into you this morning? No more days off if this is how you come back."

Betty tried to join in with the banter. But couldn't. All through the meal she worried that Mrs. Thorley would say something, especially when Dora cackled, "Man trouble. That's what's wrong with her. You mark my words."

Soon, but not soon enough for Betty, they were clearing away the pots, and Jenny and Dora had gone back to their respective jobs.

"Now tell me about Walter."

So finally Betty could unburden herself, and she found it a relief to talk about it to someone. When she'd finished Mrs. Thorley said, "I see. We wondered what had happened to that lad. Well Betty if you take my advice, you keep it to yourself. Especially, don't let Dora know. You've seen how she is with Jenny. And I know Jenny's your friend but, she can't keep a secret. It's obvious you'll want to talk about things. But I'd be careful who you talk to. People won't mean harm but it won't feel like that to you."

"I know, and thanks for keeping quiet when they were both here. You're right, I'd rather not say anything to Jenny, at the moment. She'd definitely tell Dora."

You're right there, girl. It'd help take the heat off her and her young man."

Betty laughed self-consciously. "It's not that..., you know... about Walter..." Betty stammered, lost for words.

"I understand." She squeezed Betty's shoulder.

"Well, we've never been out or anything." Betty stumbled on, trying to make some sense of her feelings in her own head. "I'm sure Walter would be embarrassed if anything was said. You should have seen him at the fair."

They both laughed now. "He's a shy lad that's for sure. I've known him since he was a toddler. He's a good lad though Betty." Suddenly serious.

"Yes I know."

They both returned to work. Betty, washed and, dried the breakfast dishes and put them away. Once that was done she filled the kettle and put it back on the hob, where eventually she could hear it singing, as she waited for Walter to return.

CHAPTER SIX.

Walter, true to his word brought up the vegetables in a barrow. She helped him unload it as she explained, in more detail, what had happened. She said she was surprised Mrs. Cohen hadn't told him, but then realised that he'd been too shy to go to the stall and ask for her.

He then, in turn, explained he'd been busy building a dovecote and so his brother David had been given the job of delivering the veg. The dovecote, now being finished, he was back on vegetable duty. He said David had mentioned a new kitchen girl, but he never for one moment thought it could be her. He blushed, crimson, as he said it.

They talked for a while, neither wanting to leave the other's company, until Mrs. Thorley opened the kitchen door. It was only then that they realised the barrow was empty.

"I need some onions, Walter." She said imperiously.

"I'll get some right away, Mrs. Thorley." He stumbled as he tried to turn the barrow in too tight a space.

"When you bring them up you can show Betty where they go. So knock on the door."

He nodded, but didn't dare speak in case he laughed out loud. He couldn't believe his luck.

"He'll bring the biggest barrow of onions you'll have ever seen. You mark my words."

Betty grinned. She nodded, agreeing with Mrs. Thorley. If he didn't she'd want to know why, she thought to herself.

"You know where they go in the cellar don't you Betty?"

She nodded, remembering her tour on her second day in the job.

"Don't be too long. I want to make a trifle for the dinner tomorrow."

Betty kissed her on her flour dusted cheek. "Give over." It was her turn to blush now. But secretly she was pleased.

Mrs. Thorley was right, though, How Walter ever managed to push the barrow remains a mystery to this day, but he did. He pushed it to the door of the cellar and then he brought a string of onions to the kitchen door. Mrs. Thorley took them from him and then sent the two of them off to unload the overloaded barrow.

"When you've done that, Walter, leave your boots on the step and come in for a cuppa," she shouted to the two receding backs. "And don't be all day," she added as an afterthought.

As they unloaded the barrow, its sides straining under the load, she passing the onions to Walter who hung them on nails knocked into a board fixed to the wall for that specific purpose, Walter explained his duties. She didn't have the heart to tell him that Mrs. Thorley had already told her what the family did, so she just listened as he talked. The family had a cottage along the lane, he was saying now; his older brother Albert had a cottage also. He'd just got married and the Major let Albert and his new bride have a cottage. He was very good like that averred Walter. He was good a man to work for. He looked after his men, so said Walter's father. There weren't many like him about today. Walter was gabbling, she decided. She remembered her speech earlier in the day and hoped it wasn't as bad as Walter's.

Slowly as the barrow emptied and the wall filled up Walter managed to stop talking about work and they agreed to meet if they finished work in time, and he would take her to see the dovecote he'd constructed. He'd still to finish painting it, he warned, but he was hopeful that with the help of his father and brothers they could get it erected before spring. Then, hopefully his doves would take to it and would use it to nest in next year. They'd just finished making these arrangements when Jenny called from the kitchen that tea was made. They looked down at the long empty barrow, "I've loads more to bring up," he said conspiratorially.

She laughed and ran back to the kitchen. He followed, taking ages to remove his muddy boots as he'd been ordered.

When he entered the kitchen, Betty and her three friends were already seated and drinking. "If you'd a' been much longer it'd been cold." Said Dora nudging Jenny. "I wondered why it was taking so long to hang up a few onions."

"Leave the lad alone. Take no notice, Walter, and drink your tea. Is it hot enough?"

Walter nodded picking up his drink, the mug, shiny white in his grubby hands. He was uncomfortable at the table surrounded by the women but he made his drink last as long as he dared so that he could sneak looks at Betty. She on the other hand never seemed to look in his direction at all.

Once the fun had gone out of embarrassing Walter, Dora began to talk of other things and soon the four women were engrossed in conversation about general household things which meant nothing to Walter and he relaxed a little and never took his eyes off Betty. Jenny certainly noticed. She decided to tell Betty that night, as she didn't think Betty had noticed Walter at all.

Too soon Walter had finished his all but cold tea and after taking an age to put on his boots, he took his barrow and went off down the garden path whistling.

"Something's cheered him up," nodded Dora sagely, looking in Betty's direction.

Betty ignored her and began to clear away the pots.

***

Betty finished work at five thirty. Unusually early for her. She was sure Mrs. Thorley had arranged it. She took off her cap and put her outdoor coat on over her uniform. It was the beginning of October and the evenings were getting cold. She opened the kitchen door and then realised she and Walter hadn't arranged a meeting place. She needn't have worried as he was leaning on the wall of the meat room his back to the door, looking towards the lane. She ran down the path and he turned as she reached him. They looked at each other in the low evening sunlight, neither spoke, then he led her toward the door in the high wall around the garden. "This is where I work. We've got a workshop in here." He couldn't think of anything else to say. He'd been trying all day, since they made the arrangement to meet, to think of what they could talk about. That was the best he could do. He felt so inadequate.

They walked nervously, self-consciously keeping a distance between themselves, down the long path to the workshop. All the time Walter was pointing out the different fruits and vegetables they grew. It was as if he couldn't bear the silence, he talked so much. He pointed out the large greenhouses where they started off the young plants, and where they grew tomatoes, cucumbers and other more exotic plants even through the winter. He turned towards a lean-to building and Betty realised they were heading to the back of the wall where the waste bins for the kitchen stood. She mentioned this and Walter agreed, "All this time you were working here, talking to our David and I was in here, only a couple of feet away and I didn't know." He grinned foolishly and opened the rough-hewn door.

On the floor of the workshop was a six-sided dovecote. It lay on one of its sides, and Walter had painted the upper half of it white. "Tomorrow when it's properly dry I'll turn it over and do the rest." He explained. The shallow, pointed roof of the dovecote was covered in tar paper to keep it waterproof. "I'll paint the roof last." Each of its six sides had two entrances, one above the other, so that the doves could get inside. By an ingenious method, using rods and eyelets Walter had devised a way of taking off alternate sides for cleaning out the cote. He explained all this to Betty. The floor of the cote had a square socket protruding from it. This was about eighteen inches long and made of metal. This was the reason the dovecote was laying on its side. The socket had been made by the blacksmith so that it would take a three inch by three inch pole. This pole would be about seven or eight feet long, and would support the dovecote when it was finished. A site had already been chosen by the Major. Walter had already selected a pole with the help of the woodsman. That was his last job, to make the top of the round pole square enough to fit into the socket. Walter pointed to two bolts on the bench, and explained that they would go through holes in the metal socket and through the pole to secure the dovecote to it. When everything was ready the dovecote would become a prominent feature of the Major's garden. After this explanation Walter beamed at his creation. Betty was impressed.

"Who..." she began.

"I built it in my spare time. I heard the Major talking to my dad one day saying he'd seen one and liked the idea. So I built it. There was an old wagon by the blacksmiths. He told me it was scrap and gave me permission to use the timber. So that's what it's built out of. The Major's seen it now and he thinks its champion, as I said he's already decided where he wants it to go."

"How did you do it? Did the Major get a plan for one?" Betty's dad was good with his hands but she couldn't imagine him making anything like the dovecote she was looking at.

Walter looked bemused. "A plan?" The thought had never occurred to him. "There's one in Shireoaks. We went there once and I saw that one. I took notice how it was made. I like making things so I take notice when I see something I like. It's just knocking wood together. It's nothing special. I do most of the maintenance around here. I like that sort of work." He finished lamely.

"It is Walter. I don't know many people who could make that."

He appeared to be about to speak but thought better of it and just looked at the brick floor of the building and was quiet.

I've embarrassed him, she thought. "It's getting dark." She hated to say it. "I'd better get back, it's a big day tomorrow. The Major's got guests coming and we've all sorts of fancy things to make."

Walter looked crestfallen, but he nodded and showed her out of his workshop. "Will I see you again?" he asked at the last minute as they reached the kitchen door.

"If you want too."

He touched her hand and ran off down the path without telling her whether he wanted to or not. She gathered from his rapid escape that he did.

That night as she drifted off to sleep Jenny told her that she thought Walter liked her. Betty thought to herself, I like Walter too. That night she dreamed of doves.

Over the coming months Betty became more integrated into the staff at the Manor. She met the Major and his wife and found them to be, as everyone had said, fair and honest. She became assistant cook and on certain days when there were no guests Betty did all the cooking and Mrs. Thorley, who at last had become Audrey, did the preparation. Roles reversed. She saw her parents on her days off and occasionally the Cohens, still her greatest friends. Even her mother now accepted the situation somewhat begrudgingly. It was difficult for her to let her little girl go. Although she was very proud of her, and, although she never told Betty, Mrs. Burton spoke very highly of her.

The situation with Walter was much the same, although now the couple were officially courting. They had been a couple for so long even Dora had stopped commenting on it. Their affair was slow burning. They went walking most evenings after work. When they both had time off together they would go to the pictures, but that meant a bus ride to the town, as the village didn't boast anything as grand as a cinema. Or they would go to the local dance, although Walter wasn't much of a dancer; they would stumble around the floor holding each other tightly, which they both enjoyed doing. So they loved the dances.

They made plans for the future, which they enjoyed even more than the dances. Talking about when they had a house, furniture and when they were really daring, when they had a family and names for the little ones. Their favourite fantasy of all was the wedding. What a day that would be, who would they invite? Who would come? What would she wear? What a great day that would be. Flowers, it would be a spring wedding because she loved the spring flowers, and confetti, there would be confetti, she'd seen it on the films and she wanted it at her wedding. Yes she'd have confetti.

They would kiss and Betty would be walking down the aisle, in her mind's eye after those dates. As Jenny prattled on in the next bed, she dreamt of that day. Those were the best times.

They made plans for their future. The political situation, all the talk of war in the newspapers didn't affect them in the least. They were deeply in love and could think only of themselves and their future.

It was the fourth of August 1913.

CHAPTER SEVEN.

Betty was now seventeen and Walter sixteen. They had walked into the village. It was a Saturday and both had the day off. They were looking forward to a full day in each other's company. The sky was blue and cloudless and the sun was shining. In the air Walter pointed out the doves circling above them, tumbling he called it.

Walter had taken his jacket off and was carrying it slung over his shoulder when they heard the sound of the church bells pealing out to tell the world that some happy couple had just got married. They made their way along the path that led to the church and watched as the couple were covered in confetti as they ran the gauntlet of friends and family to the waiting, decorated pony and trap. They watched as the laughing couple were driven off chased by friends still throwing confetti, which swirled around in their wake.

Betty remembered her dreams of confetti at her own wedding and the rest of the day was spent, thanks to the wedding they'd witnessed, planning their own big day. They walked and planned. As evening drew on they made their way to Betty's parent's house, where Walter formally asked for Betty's hand. Neither of them envisaged any problem. Walter had been accepted by Betty's parents, welcomed even, when they had started seeing each other, so they both thought it would be a formality when they entered the cottage.

Betty's father agreed to the betrothal, but when they said they wanted to get married straight away, he said he thought they should wait a while longer. Both parents thought a longer engagement was necessary. They were still very young, they had their whole lives ahead of them, so why rush into marriage. After a few tears and some discussion the couple agreed that Betty's parents were probably right. That didn't mean for one minute that they wouldn't get married, said Walter, with Betty in full agreement, but they would have to wait a while longer.

Betty's parents waved the couple off as they set out on the walk back to the Manor to tell Walter's parents what had been decided. They laughed at the intensity of the young couple as they remembered their own courting days. "I hope they don't see another wedding on their way home." joked Betty's father.

Walter's parents agreed with Betty's parents, and they accepted that the couple would be getting married. Walter's mother told them she thought of them as being engaged already, even though the formality of the ring hadn't happened yet, she said pointedly, looking at Walter. This statement placated the love-struck couple no end and their day off ended happily after all.

So life at the Manor went on as usual. Walter's dovecote was raised, under the Major's supervision, and his wife laid on a little party for the staff while the thing was struggled into position. No one expected it to be so heavy, or for it to take so much trouble, getting it plumb, but finally all was done to the Major's satisfaction. The Major's wife called the party an inauguration. Betty and Audrey had made lemonade and sandwiches while the Major and his men enjoyed a barrel of beer, delivered from the local hostelry. The inauguration turned into a lovely evening enjoyed immensely by all who attended.

The doves (the Major acquired some white, fan-tails) took to the cote after a little persuasion, which entailed fastening them into the cote for a week or so until it became home to them. The Major had Walter make a bench, which was positioned under an ancient elm tree which stood nearby. Anyone walking in the grounds could sit and watch the doves as they flew in and out of the cote. It became a favourite place for the lovers. Walter began to call Betty his little dove. She protested saying it was silly but secretly she loved his pet name for her, almost as much, she realised, as she had grown to love him.

The idyllic world at the Manor continued into a wet and cold winter. Betty and Audrey spent a lot of time making broths and soups for the men who worked outside throughout this time. All sorts of jobs still had to be done despite the elements. Animals had to be cleaned and fed. As did the fowls. Walter was always cold during this period because he spent so much time ensuring his charges were well looked after. Even so he lost a number of them to the cold.

Winter slowly became spring and with the spring came a change in the weather. The rain became warmer as one wit put it. It was reported in the southern newspapers that temperatures in the south were soaring, but further north it was still wet. Which hampered the planting, both on the farm and in the garden. Under the glass in the greenhouses though, work went on apace. Betty was in the meat shed one day. She was skinning a rabbit; she'd found out what the nails in the bench were for. The animal's skin was removed, using the nails to pull it off. She hated this part of her job,

But as Audrey had once told her, it had to be done. She heard Audrey calling from the kitchen door. She finished what she was doing and carried the rabbit, now cleaned, into the kitchen.

"Tea's up," said Audrey, pouring. Dora and Jenny were already drinking.

"Dora's just saying that it's in the paper that Franz Ferdinand's been assassinated in Sarajevo," Audrey said knowledgeably.

"Who's Franz Ferdinand?" asked Betty, pulling out a chair and sitting down, after placing the rabbit on the draining board by the sink ready for washing.

Audrey looked at Dora who shrugged.

"Where's Sarajevo?" asked Jenny.

"I'll let you read the paper," said Dora. "It's a couple of days old though."

No one bothered to read it. But now the countdown had begun.

***

After that day the weather changed for the better. The outdoor work at the Manor was able to pick up and soon planting, both in the fields and in the gardens was almost back to normal. Thanks to the glasshouses the plants in the garden were almost where they should have been for the time of year.

The Major was spending an inordinate amount of time away from the house. Usually at planting time and harvest, he and Mr. Burton would have been out riding around the estate keeping a watchful eye on the work. But not this year. It was Mr. Burton alone, in his guise as estate manager, that was out there, running things.

Not that many people noticed. With the amount of work to catch up on everyone was too busy. June became July and the weather was becoming changeable again. Not in the south, as Audrey informed anyone who would listen. Her cousin, who lived near Brighton wrote to her telling her how glorious it was there.

Betty and Walter still enjoyed their evening walks when the weather allowed. They still talked of getting married but now it was next year. Walter was saving up for an engagement ring. He'd already spoken to Mr. Cohen. They had reached the stage in their relationship where it was allowed Walter would kiss her goodnight on the kitchen steps as they parted for the night. Betty loved to say goodnight.

Jenny and her farmhand had already got engaged, and she was always showing off her engagement ring, much to Betty's chagrin. They had bought the ring at Mr. Cohen's and Jenny was a little put out when she found that Betty knew the Cohen's well. Betty placated her by telling her that they were the best jeweller's in town by far, and showing her the ring Mr. Cohen had made for her when she left their employ to work at the Manor.

Jenny told Betty, in confidence, which Betty knew meant everyone knew, that her and her young man were planning on getting married in the August of next year, which was when she and Walter planned to get engaged. Late into the night the two friends planned a double celebration, a wedding and an engagement on the same day. They both went to sleep dreaming of that big day. For once Jenny wasn't talking.

The following day as Betty prepared breakfast and Dora was pouring tea, Audrey being engaged in talks with Mrs. Burton, the Major was reading in his *Times* about Russia mobilising its troops and martial law being declared in Germany. The staff knew nothing of these events and when Audrey returned she was talking about making a mushroom soup; her cousin had sent her a new recipe she wanted to try out. Life carried on as normal.

Betty and Walter, after the madness of the last few weeks planting, had a weekend off, together. This was a luxury, more so as the Major was away again in London and usually

67

when the Major was away Mr Burton didn't like people taking time off. But because they'd had such a torrid time lately catching up with the work, he turned a blind eye. They spent one day with Walter's parents at their cottage. This was situated on the Major's land near the farm gates. There was a row of nine tied cottages for the use of the estate workers. Walter's brother had one as well as his parents. They stood on the lane which led to the farm and the stables. Opposite the cottages stood an avenue of ancient beech trees and in the autumn Albert would allow his pigs access to the fields in which the beeches stood to feed on the beech mast which the pigs thought a great delicacy. Betty wrinkled her nose as Walter told her this. Walter loved to see her do that. As Walter and Betty walked down the lane towards the cottages a strangely dressed woman appeared around the bend walking towards them. She was tall and slim; she wore a long reddish, brown skirt that shimmered as she moved and which reached almost to her ankles. On her feet she wore sandals, and a wide, black belt at her waist over her Paisley blouse sported a large silver buckle. On her head she wore a red, silk scarf, fastened pirate-style, which covered her ears and where it was fastened behind her head it hung down her back to her waist. Over her arm she carried a deep woven basket filled with silks and black cat lucky charms. In her free hand she clasped a white clay pipe, broken to a stump. As she passed them walking quickly, on her way to the village, she nodded in a friendly manner, and clamped the stump of the pipe stem between her lips. The smoke followed in her wake as she walked off down the lane.

Betty was fascinated by this creature. She'd never seen anything like her in the whole of her, admittedly, sheltered life, and she turned to stop and stare as the woman disappeared around the bend. "Who was that?" she exclaimed.

Walter stopped, waiting for Betty to catch up, "She's from the gypsy camp. The Major lets them stop in the top pasture when they're here."

"She doesn't look like the gypsies I saw at the fair."

"That's because she's a real Romany gypsy. They travel selling whatever they can. They make things; jewellery and the like, lucky charms, pegs. They sell them door to door. They'll tell your fortune if you'll let them." He laughed. "The Major lets them stay on the understanding they don't come pestering around our doors. There's about six caravans this time. We think it's just one family."

"Have you been up to see them?" saked Betty truly interested.

"No. But Albert's been up there. He's seen them, and their horses and caravans. He says they're really friendly."

They had arrived at Walter's parents' house now. Betty could smell the freshly baked bread Walter's mum was just taking out of the oven as they walked down the path to the door. The cottages were similar in design to Betty's parents' place. They were two up two down with a shared rear yard and a chemical toilet each at the bottom of the shared yard. The difference being that Walter's parents' house was built of the local stone while Betty's parents' place was brick. Walter's mum had the front window open because the room was so hot with the stove fired up for her baking. So they sat outside in the front garden, under the open window, looking at the beeches while the room cooled down. Betty noticed the bench was similar to the one near the dove cote and surmised Walter had made this one also. It was very pleasant looking out over the fields, through the great trees, listening to the breeze as it whispered through the branches.

"What are you two up to today then?" asked Walter's mum.

Betty told her about the gypsy they'd seen as they walked down the lane.

"Arthur said he's seen them. I hope they don't come around here."

"Mam's superstitious about them. She thinks they bring bad luck," laughed Walter.

She flicked Walter with the tea towel she invariably carried (Betty had never seen her without it) as he sat in front of them on the neatly trimmed lawn. She was laughing but Betty sensed her unease even as she laughed.

They ate bread and home-made jam sandwiches and talked about the people who lived in the other cottages. Of the nine cottages eight were currently occupied. Albert had the end one. Then came Walter's parents. Next door was Amos Clamp. He lived alone and was the cow man. He provided all the milk and beef. Next door to Amos lived Mrs. Asquith, Walter's mum's good friend, and her husband Eric. He was the estate's blacksmith. He had made the socket which was under Walter's dovecote. He and Walter got on well, despite their age difference, both being practical men good with their hands. The next cottage was empty. This was the one Betty and Walter coveted, and one of their reasons for visiting Walter's mum today. So that they could see the place. Mr. and Mrs. Grogan came next. He was a general labourer on the farm and a giant of a man. As strong as an ox. Mrs. Grogan had confided in Mrs. Asquith and through her to Walter's mum that she was worried about her youngest son who'd joined the army. She was afraid there was going to be a war. Walter shook his head in disbelief, "She worries too much; Billy'll be all right. There won't be a war. Our government's not that stupid."

The three of them nodded but Walter's mum was quiet, thinking about her neighbour's son if war did break out. It seemed now from the newspapers that it was a possibility.

Mrs. Grogan's eldest son lived next door to her with his wife of one year. She was pregnant with their first child and all the women in the row were knitting for her. Eli Williams widower and woodsman, lived next door to the young married couple. He coppiced the Major's woods and maintained all the hedgerows on the estate. He had a young lad from the village help him occasionally. He also supplied the logs to the Manor. The last cottage was occupied by Noah Jones and his wife, Nellie. Noah was the gamekeeper. A taciturn man, he and his wife were very religious people and didn't mix with the others along the row. They kept their own counsel, but were always on hand if anyone needed help.

That was everyone, but really the only property Betty and Walter were interested in was the empty one. Sandwiches and tea finished Betty helped Mrs. Blower (Betty couldn't yet call her 'Mam', so she was still 'Mrs. Blower', much to Walter's amusement) clear up. Then they went and looked through the windows of the empty cottage before bidding goodbye to Walter's mum and wandering off to look at the gypsy encampment. As they walked, hand in hand, they talked about what they would do if they were lucky enough to get the cottage.

That day went by too quickly, and Sunday seemed to be over in a sun-drenched flash for the two lovers. It was a lovely day which they spent walking to the village to visit Betty's parents and then the Cohens, but all too soon the goodnight kiss at the kitchen door was but a memory on Betty's lips, the weekend was over, and she was in bed dreaming of Walter and her cottage.

Monday and Betty was back at work. She and Audrey were talking about the visit to Mrs. Blower's cottage, a woman that Audrey knew well and liked. Inevitably the conversation came round to the empty cottage and Betty's ambition to live there.

"You'd better reel that Walter in then, if you want that cottage. They go to first come first served you know. Jenny will be looking for somewhere to live when she gets wed. Have you thought of that?"

Betty hadn't and said so.

The two worked on in silence. Betty worrying now about the cottage and wondering if Walter would have an idea about what to do. Tea time arrived and it was a subdued Dora that entered the kitchen closely followed by Jenny. Betty couldn't look at Jenny at first, but then pulled herself round. 'First come first served' Audrey had said. But she didn't want to make it a race to the altar. She would just have to see what happened. It was no good dwelling on it.

"You're quiet Dora. What's up?"

Betty had been so involved in her own thoughts she hadn't noticed her two friends were both very subdued.

"I've just had a look at the Major's paper," said Jenny.

"She wishes she hadn't now," continued Dora for Jenny.

"Who's Sir Edward Grey?" Jenny asked.

They all looked to Audrey." I think he's Foreign Secretary. Why?"

"That's right. That's what it said." Jenny addressed Dora.

"It says in the paper that he's told parliament we're at war with Germany." Dora said as Jenny stared silently at her mug of tea.

The four friends looked at each other in disbelief. "War," said Audrey. Her eyes filled up. "It must be wrong. Are you sure?"

Jenny just nodded.

Betty told them then about the Grogan's youngest boy being in the army. Audrey shook her head. "The poor woman must be beside herself."

War was the sole topic of conversation in the kitchen that day. War was officially declared on the fourth of August, the government having failed to receive notice assuring Belgian neutrality, and citing 'a moral obligation' to our allies. Of course this news took a while to filter through to the kitchen, with the ladies waiting for Jenny to catch a glimpse of the Major's newspaper.

Much to the surprise of the female staff most of the men around the Manor were cock-a-hoop at the prospect.

"We'll teach them buggers a lesson," "We'll show them Jerries," and "They'll be begging for mercy by Christmas," were some of the jingoistic cries heard from some of the more voluble men around the estate.

It appeared from the newspaper headlines that most of the country felt the same way. "What's wrong with everybody?" asked Audrey of no one in particular one day. "Has the world gone mad?"

Apparently it had.

Soon young men were volunteering in droves. They could be seen marching off to training camps, in wild far flung corners of Britain, from every village, town and city in the land. Even Mrs. Grogan's fears for her son were tempered with pride when he came home on his embarkation leave in his smart khaki uniform. The Major paid them a visit to see the boy and to personally shake his hand and thank him. The boy told all at that meeting that all the recruits had been told at the last training camp, that hostilities were expected to be over by Christmas. The Germans, they'd been assured, did not want war. He begged his mother not to worry. He told her, privately, when the Major had left, that he was looking forward to his voyage. He'd see other places. He'd travel, which was something he'd always wanted to do. His mates would be with him, he'd made some good friends in his troop, and he'd been assured by the officers that when they all came home they'd have a big beano at the camp. He believed what the officers had told him completely and he seemed so certain in what he said that she began to believe him. He told all the neighbours in the cottages about his experiences at the training camp he'd been to near Whitby. His enthusiasm was contagious and Walter and his friends were more than a little envious of young Grogan as he waved goodbye to his mother and left the Manor to go and fight. Even the Major, who laid on a trap to take him to the station to meet his comrades rode down to the estate gates, on his favourite horse with Mr. Burton, to wave him off and bid him Godspeed.

So it was that the first soldier from the Manor left to fight in 'The war to end war'. It was the eleventh of August. Exactly one week after hostilities had been declared.

After that momentous day, the weather worsened for some time and thoughts went back to work on the Manor. The harvest was almost upon them and there was a lot of work to occupy everyone's mind. But the war would not go away. It was forever in the headlines and in letters from friends and family along the south coast, where more of the troops seemed to be stationed. The papers gave lists of victories and sometimes mentioned casualties, but not often. The maimed and killed were never mentioned. So the year went on.

Christmas came and went, the magic time when it was all supposed to be over. But there was no end in sight. Still the whole country, according to the partisan press was upbeat about the war. It was only five months since it began, they crowed, at the end of December, the pages full of stories of Allied victories.

One day, the Major called for his men to assemble on the drive at the front of the house. This was an unprecedented call. The men had never been called together before. They all met after the day's work on the gravel turning area in front of the white pillared portico which was the entrance to the Manor House. The Major arrived accompanied by Mr. Burton.

Both were mounted on their favourite horses. The Major was in full dress uniform. It was February the first 1915.

He addressed the men from his mount; the horse pawed the gravel as the Major looked down from his saddle at the group. "As some of you may already know Captain Villiers has taken some of his men to fight in France." Captain Villiers' family owned the estate bordering the Major's own. Over the years there had been some friendly rivalry between the two estates. Especially at the local livestock show. But this was something different.

"This patriotic move," continued the Major a little stuffily, "has left him short-handed, and so I've told him that we will do our best to help out where we can. Now I know some of you have been talking about joining up, like young Grogan did. I've heard from his mother, only this morning, by the way, that the boy is doing all right. He can't say where he is, as you can appreciate, but he says that he and his comrades have given Jerry a bloody nose on more than one occasion. So I say three cheers for young Grogan and his chums!" The Major raised a cheer and the crowd joined in with gusto. They cheered so loudly that Jenny, who was working upstairs at the time, looked out of the landing window to see what the noise was about. She was therefore able to report to the ladies in the kitchen what she'd seen at tea time, much to Dora's chagrin, and Jenny's delight.

"And so to the second reason I've called you all here today." The Major looked across at Mr. Burton and he nodded imperceptibly." You may have noticed my absence last year during harvest time when Mr. Burton here shouldered the responsibility of running the place single-handedly." He looked at Burton and continued, "For which I am eternally grateful." Burton again nodded. "However, during this time I was not idle. Myself and some colleagues from the army, realising that war was inevitable, decided to raise a company of men; men we knew from our own time in the forces. Men we could trust to do everything in their power to bring this war to swift and suitable conclusion." This raised another cheer from his audience, now hanging on his every word, which he deprecatingly waved down. "This company is now formed and we need some volunteers to swell its ranks and make it into the formidable fighting force we know it can be." Every hand went into the air as these last words were spoken, peer pressure forced up any waverers. The only man to keep his hand down was Noah Jones.

The Major smiled and he and Mr. Burton nodded knowingly to each other, as their horses skittered on the gravel at the unusual movement in front of them. The Major waved the raised arms down. "I expected no less from men of your calibre. But as I have just said, I've promised to help out our neighbour. Soldiers need to eat too you know." This raised a laugh from the crowd. "We can't fight on empty bellies. So those who stay behind will be doing sterling work also." There was some muttering among the gathering.

"I won't be taking any married men, I need you here." For a moment there was uproar, and the Major thought he'd lost his audience, but finally he managed to calm the crowd down. He hadn't realised how strongly feelings were running. "This is not because I don't want to take you, but as I've said I need you here. This work is equally as important as fighting. More so even, because we have to feed everyone left at home too. Not just the men fighting. They want something to come back to. Now I can't stop you signing on in town. That's up to you, and I can quite understand if you do. But I just hope that you don't for the reasons I've just given." This reasoning seemed to placate the men, and the Major carried on quickly while he had them quiet. "I need skilled men here with two estates to harvest; yours will be a difficult enough job. It will take all those left behind to do it. I will only take single men. I don't want anyone with marriage plans or who is engaged either, you will have other things on your mind. Single, unattached men only. So all those I've just discounted, I want you to fall out and go to Mr. Burton." Mr. Burton was now dismounting. He tied up his mount to a rose bush and walked away from the Major towards the corner of the building. "He will explain the division of labour now and how it's going to work with the Villierses. The rest of you come to me." He stayed mounted so that he could see who was there. He looked out over the twenty-five faces left below him. "Billy," he pointed to a tall youth at the back of the crowd with thinning straw coloured hair, "I thought you were engaged to Jenny? Come on lad. Get over to Mr. Burton."

He shamefacedly sloped off and joined the other group. And so it went on for the next hour until the Major had whittled down his group to twenty men, one of whom was Walter.

"Now, boys, I want you to go home and think about what you're volunteering for. Talk it over with your loved ones, I don't want anyone to have misgivings, or who may feel they've got it wrong. I admire Noah Jones, he has convictions and nothing will sway him. That's the sort of man I admire. I may not agree with him but I admire him for sticking to his guns under what must be tremendous pressure. I want the same from you. It doesn't matter what anyone else thinks or says, do what you think is right. Now off you go. Anyone wanting to fight, come back tomorrow at this time and I'll have someone here from the company to sign you up. Then on Friday you'll be off to training camp. I know its short notice, but the sooner we get over there the sooner we'll be back. Now give your decision some serious thought in the intervening time. Good luck, men!" With that he turned his horse and rode over to where Mr. Burton was talking to the other group of men.

The young men he'd left stood talking for some time until the Major told them to go home, whence they slowly dispersed, leaving in groups of twos and threes. Walter left with a lad from the village called Jonas, who worked in the gardens with his father. Jonas was excited by the whole event and looked upon it as a great adventure. Walter could see already that no one was going to talk Jonas out of going. Walter heard someone calling him and he turned to see who it was. It was his father, so he waited for him to catch up, and Jonas walked on, to join up with the group in front of them.

"What are you thinking of, Walter?" he asked without preamble as he approached the youth.

"What do you mean, Dad?"

"Well you're supposed to be engaged to Betty, aren't you? What about all this wedding talk we've been hearing lately?"

"It was you and Mam told us to wait."

"Your mam looks upon you as engaged and so do I."

"Yes but we're not are we? Not yet."

"What do you think the lass will say? You wanting to join up without talking it over with her. It's not right you know. She's been making plans. I've seen her looking at the cottage near us. You an' all, lad. There's two of you in the bargain."

They were walking through the garden now on the way home.

"I'll talk it over with her tonight when I see her. I haven't said I'm definitely going yet," Walter said angrily knowing deep down his dad was right.

Walter's father nodded, knowing what sort of pressure the lad would be under as soon as others in the group started to sign up. He held his tongue, understanding that anything he said now would only push Walter closer to joining, which was something neither his mother nor himself wanted. Betty he felt certain would feel the same.

CHAPTER EIGHT.

That night after many words and tears from his mother, over a tea of bacon and cabbage, with thick slices of his mother's home-made bread to fill him up, Walter went to meet Betty at their special place: the bench near the dovecote. She was already there when he arrived, watching the white doves as they flew in and out of the openings, cooing to each other in the gentle way that they had. They kissed and he sat down next to her, unable to look at her. He knew straight away that something was wrong. She was quiet, pensive, scuffing at the worn, sparse grass in front of the bench with the toe of her shoe.

"What's wrong?" he asked, already knowing the answer.

"Jenny says you've joined up."

"How does Jenny know?" He frowned, perplexed.

"She watched the Major's meeting from the upstairs window. She says you were with the ones singled out."

Walter realised what had happened and decided he'd better come straight to the point. He told her everything he could remember about what had been said. About it being a special group and that the Major would be there with them. He made sure to mention the assurances that the campaign would be short lived and that all the boys who went would stay together. He told her about Grogan's letter and about how well he was doing, and how proud the Major was of him, being from the estate. Finally he mentioned, what he hoped would ensure her approval, the cottage. "When I come back, we'll get engaged straight away and I'll ask the Major for the next cottage that comes available. I'll tell him we're planning our wedding around that. He won't be able to say no, will he, after I've been away fighting with his troop?"

Betty wept. She said nothing. She just sat staring at the patchy ground, and wept. Her tears, with her dreams, rolling down her cheeks. Her tears dropped, unwiped, from her chin and onto her lap where she screwed up her handkerchief between her constantly moving fingers. Walter had never seen her cry before. He didn't know what to do. He thought he'd worked out the perfect argument. He couldn't understand the problem. He would go away for maybe, a month, two at the most. And when he got back, there would be no argument about their youth, everyone would be caught up in their victory. So they would get engaged, and still in this time of euphoria, he would ask about the cottage. He was positive that the Major would agree. How could he not? So far as he could see the plan was fool proof. He sat silently next to Betty as she sobbed, racking sobs that tore at his heart, with no sign of them ending soon. Slowly he put his arm around her, not knowing what else to do; he sat like that as the sky darkened and evening became night. Slowly Betty's tears subsided. Now she sobbed, catching her breath like a baby until eventually she was silent in the darkness. They sat a long time like this, neither speaking. Neither knowing what to say. She leaned her head on his shoulder, as if she didn't want it to be there but had nowhere else for it to go.

It was full dark now and still Betty said nothing. It was getting cold but she didn't seem to feel it. He tried to pull her to him, but she resisted. So they sat side by side, her head uncomfortably on his shoulder until, after close to an hour she said, "You've made up your mind then?"

"I just think it'll work out better for us. That's all; if I do this. Don't you think so?"

"Oh! Walter. I don't think so. No! I don't mind waiting. If you're here, I'll wait as long as it takes. It doesn't matter as long as we're together. But I don't like this. Your going away. I don't like it at all." She stood up. He thought for one dreadful moment she was going to walk away, but she just stood looking at the dovecote in the gloom; the white birds like ghosts shuffling about as they tried to get comfortable to roost for the night, softly cooing to each other as they moved.

He felt an overpowering sense of love sweep over him as he looked at her. He knew then, at that moment how much she loved him. He wanted to take her in his arms, smother her in kisses and take her away. He didn't know where to, or why, he just felt this overpowering urge to hold her and to never let her go. What he did, was to stand next to her for a moment and then say, "Come on, dove. It's getting late. We'll talk some more tomorrow. When we've both slept on it."

She nodded and they walked together hand in hand, silently, through the garden to the kitchen door. The house appeared to be in total darkness as he kissed her goodnight for the longest time. He felt her new tears on his cheek as he turned and walked away homewards.

She entered the dark house and ran through the kitchen and up the winding staircase to her shared room, where Jenny was sitting in bed waiting for her. Betty ignored her friend, not even noticing her there, and threw herself onto her bed, where she cried softly to herself. Jenny threw back her covers and sitting on Betty's bed she patted her back, as you would a child, until the sobbing subsided. They held each other deep into the cold reaches of the night saying nothing. What was there for friends to say to each other at such a time as this?

The following day went by in a daze for Betty. She did her work automatically. Audrey didn't know what to say to her and at tea break even Dora was quiet. Audrey was surprised at Walter, but reading the newspaper headlines, she realised that the whole country had been whipped up into a kind of warlike frenzy. It was unthinkable, according to the newspapers, and even the letters she received from her cousin in Brighton, told her no one believed Britain could lose this war. Anyone taking a different line was unpatriotic. So it followed that for a young man not to want to fight made him unpatriotic. The sooner one got over to Europe and beat the Germans the sooner the world would get back to normal. That was the message Audrey was taking from the newspapers, and it was also what she believed young Walter had in his head. He wanted to get this war over, so that he could get on with his life with Betty, who was obviously, a blind man could see it, the love of his life.

Audrey didn't think Betty saw it like that at the moment though.

Walter brought up the vegetables and eggs later than usual, the lovers talked while they unloaded the barrow. There wasn't much to unload as it was February and most of the veg used at this time of year came out of storage. Although there were some early spring greens and some things from the greenhouses.

"When do you have to sign on?" she asked.

"Betty. If you don't want me to go I'll stay. If that's what you want, just say." Walter was distraught, she could see in his eyes how much he wanted to go and at that moment she loved him more than she ever thought it possible for one person to love another.

While she and Jenny lay together on the bed, she'd gone over in her mind what she would say to Walter. She'd decided she would implore him not to go, if she had to go down on her bended knees she would. She had a really bad feeling in the pit of her stomach about this, and she intended to tell him so. She thought, if she was honest with herself, she knew, she could get him to stay with her. But now that the carefully planned moment was here, she couldn't do it. Not because he so desperately wanted to go; she believed what he'd said to her the night before at the dovecote. She honestly believed he thought it would get them married earlier and get them a cottage. It was what it would do to them, and the way they felt about each other, that had changed her mind. She'd heard what Audrey had said, about what she'd been reading, over the weeks that had gone, since the start of the war, but today, when Audrey had spoken she'd really listened. Up until today it had just been background noise and it hadn't actually affecter her. It was something happening hundreds of miles away, to someone else. She and Walter had plans to make and a different life to lead, but now it did concern her and Walter. It impinged on her very soul, and it was going to take away the man she loved. She knew now that it was going to do that! If he didn't go, how would he feel, knowing that every other person he'd grown up with had gone, and fought? How would he look at her, how would he feel about her, if he stayed because she'd asked him to. He was a proud person, he wouldn't be able to look any of the boys in the eye again, if he didn't go. It would be impossible for him to continue to live here, and he would blame her. Maybe not at first, but as time wore on, the hurt would get deeper and it would open up a sore, a suppurating lesion between them, that no love could heal. Not even a love as strong as theirs could stand such a wound.

She wanted him to stay with every fibre of her being and because she did, she said, "I want to come and watch you sign on. If that's what you want to do. I'll cheer you off."

He whisked her up off the ground and swung her around. He kissed her face, her ears everywhere his lips touched while he danced around the yard, he kissed her, oblivious to anyone being there. When he stopped he realised that Dora, Audrey and Jenny were watching them from the doorway. He dropped Betty so quickly she nearly fell over. "I'll see you later, dove." And he scuttled off.

"He's going then?" said Audrey as they all went back inside.

Betty couldn't speak. She just nodded. Audrey held her as she wept again. "I just couldn't ask him to stay, Audrey. What else could I do? They're all going."

"They don't make it easy on us lass, do they? They don't make it easy." Audrey stood with Betty enfolded in her arms, swaying slowly from side to side as she had done with her own daughter when she was a child. She hummed a little tune as Betty slowly recovered her composure. Audrey thought of Betty and Walter, just children themselves, with everything to look forward to, and of her own husband lost in Africa long ago in another fruitless war when Audrey herself had been but a child, with a child of her own. A child she lost to measles, a baby girl called Edna. "It never ends," she said more to herself than to anyone else, "And those that cause it never suffer the consequences." She kissed Betty's head as she reluctantly let her go.

Dora nodded to Jenny and they quietly left the cook and her assistant alone.

That evening twenty boys signed on in the entrance hall to the Manor. True to his word the Major had brought someone with him to oversee the proceedings. This person, a colour sergeant that was acquainted with the Major told the boys that they were signing on for the duration, which he joked would not be very long if he could get an army made of men of the calibre he saw here today; "Hearts of oak," he quoted. All the boys swelled with pride at this. The sergeant stood them in a row outside after they'd all signed and ordered them to attention.

"Won't take me long to train these lads," he said to the Major who grinned widely as he looked down from his horse. All the boys' parents and girlfriends had come along to witness the ceremony. They stood and applauded as their loved ones marched a circuit of the drive, with a mixture of pride and apprehension, fear and sadness, in their collective demeanour. Betty felt physically sick as she watched Walter, grinning from ear to ear, swinging his arms back and forth as they marched around in an ungainly circle across the gravel. The colour sergeant finally called the boys to order and as they stood in line in front of him on the steps of the portico he told them that on Friday morning an army wagon would arrive to take them to the railway station in the nearby town. There they would join other young men from various areas who had also signed up and together they would all go to a training camp. He then listed clothes for them to take with them and told them they would receive army issue uniforms when they arrived at the camp.

The next three days never existed for Betty. She lived through them but even at the end of her life she could never remember them. Her next real memory was standing with Walter's mother and father at the drive gates waving goodbye to a wall of smiling faces hanging from the back of the army lorry; among the faces she remembered Walter's. It was a tearful time, but there was also a carnival atmosphere about it. The women, mothers and girlfriends cried, the men laughed and shouted, with banter and jokes. Everyone waved; a sea of arms was Betty's undying memory. Some of the men, Walter's father among them, were very solemn after the lorry turned the corner in the lane. Audrey wasn't there. She didn't want to see them go, she said to Betty when she asked her why." I don't want to wait for them to come home. You've no option girl, but I have." She never spoke of that day again.

Betty noticed Dancy Prentiss, the postman, cycling up the lane towards the cottages. The wagon carrying the boys passed him as it drove out of the gates. Another letter from Mrs. Grogan's lad she thought as she waved Walter out of sight.

The group stood and looked at the empty lane for a short while until the Major, driven by Mr. Burton left in his motor car to go to the station. He was going with the boys to the training camp and then with them onto the battlefield, as their commanding officer, wherever that was to be. Everyone waved him off. Betty noticed his wife wasn't there. And for some reason she thought of Audrey.

Slowly everyone made their separate ways back to their respective places of work. Audrey was hard at it making bread for the weekend, pummelling and pounding the dough with a vengeance, and soon the two women had slipped back into their routine. Betty asked Audrey why everyone called Dancy Prentiss, Dancy. Even his parents used the name.

Audrey laughed. It was good to see her laugh again, she'd been very taciturn since the signing on day. "When Dancy was little," she began, "he couldn't walk properly. When other kids his age were toddling Dancy just lay there; he never made any attempt to walk or even crawl. He responded to other stimulus but he just wouldn't walk. The doctor said he was lazy. 'He's just a lazy child and he will walk in his own time,' he'd said, and seemed to wash his hands of Dancy. Anyway the child never did walk or make any attempt to. Mrs. Prentiss was frantic with worry, as you can imagine. All the other kids Dancy's age were walking some were even playing out in the gardens while Dancy just lay there, doing nothing. They tried everything you could think of, but to no avail. Then one day she bought him a music box. She saw it in a shop in town and on a whim bought it. Dancy, whose given name is Joseph, by the way, loved it; he started to kick his legs straight away, as soon as they wound it up and played it to him. Almost immediately he was rolling about, and to hear her talk now he was walking the next day. But it took longer than that. To be fair though, not much longer. He would try to walk to get to the box. He loved it. They would say to him, when they played it, 'Come on Dancy, dance!' and he would totter over to them. As he grew older and better at walking he still wanted to hear the music box and he himself would call it Dancy. The music box became Dancy, and so did Joseph. The nickname stuck. He became Dancy Prentiss. Even people who've known him all his life think it's his real name. He's never been over bright hasn't Dancy. But he's perfect as the postman. He couldn't have got a better job. He'd be no-good anywhere else." She laughed. "Why do you ask? What brought that on?"

"Oh! He rode past on his bike as the lads left. Another letter for Mrs. Grogan I suppose." Audrey became quiet again and Betty wondered if she'd said something wrong.

Jenny and Dora came for their cup of tea as Audrey was getting the bread ready to prove, so it was Betty that made it. As they sat down around the big, well-scrubbed table, the smell of the first batch of bread permeated the air. It was obvious that Dora had something to say, but strangely Dora was keeping it to herself. She kept looking sideways at Jenny, Jenny was pointedly ignoring her. The conversation drifted from one inconsequential subject to another until the tea pots were washed and Betty went outside to the meat shed. Today it was to be chicken. She had to pluck and clean the bird, a job she could never get used to. When she brought the bird in it was ready, after washing for stuffing. She washed it and began to cut up onions and sage in preparation for the stuffing. She'd left some bread near the range to dry out before going out to the shed. Audrey was nowhere to be seen. Betty took the bread from the range and began to crumble it up, as Audrey entered the room. Betty caught a glimpse of Dora through the closing door as she scuttled off to her work.

"Sit down, Betty," Audrey said, her voice filled with emotion.

"Whatever's wrong, Audrey?"

Betty sat as she was bid. Audrey sat beside her and took her hand. "You remember telling me that you saw Dancy Prentiss as you waved Walter off?"

Betty nodded, wondering if something had happened to Dancy.

"Well, he was taking a telegram to the Grogan's."

Betty still didn't understand.

"Today of all days," Audrey said, as if to herself.

Betty looked at her friend uncomprehending.

"The boys going off and young Grogan... " her voice trailed off as she tried to explain.

Betty still stared at Audrey unable to comprehend what she was saying.

"He's missing in action, Betty. Presumed killed." Audrey spelled it out.

Betty sat looking over Audrey's shoulder at nothing. As she'd said, today of all days. Betty took it to be an omen. Ill fortune would dog the boys. She was certain. Positive, nothing could dissuade her. The feeling she'd had since Walter had decided to join up, was worse now, much worse. She stood allowing Audrey's hand to drop back to the table. She left the kitchen and, she didn't know how, but found herself sitting on the bench by the dovecote. The sky told her it was afternoon. How long she'd been sitting there she didn't know. She stood and walked slowly back through the garden, remembering her first walk through it with Walter telling her all the names of the various plants as they passed the beds.

Deep inside her now she knew she would never see Walter again.

When she woke up it was, for a split second, Walter, who was holding her hand and looking down at her, then she realised it was his father. "Are you all right Betty? You just keeled over. Lucky I was in the glasshouse."

"I'm sorry Mr. Blower. I don't know what happened."

"No need to be sorry love. Are you feeling unwell?"

She shook her head. "I must have sat out in the cold too long." She struggled to her feet with his help. The side of her uniform dress was muddy. She made it worse trying to brush it off and only smeared it. She began to cry.

Mr. Blower didn't know what to do, but he held her to him. "I know lass," he said, "I know."

"Mrs. Grogan..." Betty began. But Mr. Blower shushed her quiet and patted her shoulder. He smelled like her own father, tobacco, and sweat as he comforted her.

"Go on, girl, and get Audrey to make you a cup of tea. We all feel the same way today, lass. I didn't want him to go either. There's a lot to be said for Noah's point of view. But don't tell anyone. It's not the sort of thing you want to be common knowledge. Especially on the Major's payroll."

Betty didn't know what to do, so she shook his hand and left him standing on the path wondering if he'd done the right thing by telling her his feelings. Betty never forgot that moment and she looked at the bluff Mr. Blower differently from then on.

Audrey made the tea and she never mentioned Betty's abrupt disappearance at all. The chicken was in the oven and the veg was prepared and cooking away on the range. Betty knew how much work Audrey had done while she'd been absent and loved her for it all the more. She decided enough was enough. It had been her decision to agree to Walter's joining up. She could have stopped him, so she had to live with it. She had to somehow come to terms with it and pray for him to return home safely. She was not the only one in this position. There were many thousands more like her. Some much worse off. Look at Mrs. Grogan. She took a deep breath and picked up Audrey's hand. She kissed it and put it back on the table. She didn't look at Audrey as she left the room to go and change her muddy dress. When she returned it was as if nothing had happened, but both women knew that at that moment Betty had grown up.

There was a funeral for the Grogans' son. Everyone knew that the coffin was empty. There was nothing to bury. It was a service of remembrance. The whole village turned out; it appeared he had been a popular lad. Strangers stood outside the small church, as it could not accommodate all who came to remember the first soldier killed from the area. Then everything went back to normal, or what passed for normal in these strange times.

***

With the two estates to run the women were called upon to do some men's jobs. So when work in the kitchen was slack, (there were no dinner parties now) Audrey and Betty found themselves occasionally helping with the planting in the fields. The work was hard, but it was a welcome change.

***

The highlight of Betty's week was the arrival of Walter's letters. His letters were full of the places he'd seen on his travels. He mentioned Whitby and places in the Dales. He said they'd done lots of keep fit classes and exercises, which he found boring and he said they still hadn't got their uniforms yet, although they had been promised them soon. They had to wear something blue he said which made them look like postmen. She didn't understand that at all. He said they had cardboard cap badges too. He mentioned in one letter Whitby had been shelled by German warships. That was around Christmas time. Some of the locals had told him this. His physical training was to take three months, then he would be going somewhere else for firearms training. They were being assessed he said, all the time, continual assessment, the Major called it, to see where they could best be used. Betty thought it made him sound like a piece of equipment and not like a man at all. He mentioned seeing the Major on more than one occasion, so it appeared he was at the camp with the men. Walter mentioned also that the Major was trying to get the men into barracks, as at the moment they were under canvas, whatever that meant. Walter had picked up some strange terminology in the army, she grinned to herself. His letters were full of enthusiasm though, and she got the feeling from them that he was enjoying the training although he said he was bored a lot of the time. She liked the ending of the letters best, and read those parts over and over again when she was on her own. The parts where he told her how much he missed her and how he thought about her every day and dreamed of their wedding day, then he signed every letter with, 'to my dove', and lots of kisses. She kept all his letters in a drawer next to her bed.

She told Audrey about the shelling of Whitby: Audrey had stopped reading the papers calling them propaganda sheets, so she hadn't known about the attack. Slowly, though as the months passed Walters letters became less about what he was doing and more about what he wanted to do when he came home. The letters became more personal and more about their future. He had to be careful what he wrote he said, because his letters, along with everyone else's were censored. In her letters to him she tried to remain strong, but occasionally, she couldn't help herself and she then wrote telling him how much she missed him and wished he would come home. She hated to do this, but it was always after she'd posted the letter, and not before it had gone that she felt like that. She longed for him to come home on leave.

One day she received a letter saying that all post was to be sent to an army PO Box number as mail to Private Walter Blower would now be forwarded to his unit abroad. Walter had gone overseas and he'd never let her know.

CHAPTER NINE.

Walter had completed his training and the group, under the Major's supervision, had gone to Wales, where they had received further training. They had now all got their ill-fitting uniforms and boots. Walter had related this in letters to his parents and to Betty, but the mail from Wales had got mixed up and been sent south. The Major had then taken his men to a coastal port and they had been given one day's embarkation leave. Most of the boys didn't know what embarkation leave meant and it was only when they left port, Dover as it happened, for France that they realised they were on their way to the front. There had been some talk about some of the men, men like Walter who were good with their hands, being transferred to a place called Richborough, where a lot of building work was taking place, but the Major had quashed this idea as he had promised the men they would stay together.

All the men wrote to their loved ones explaining what had happened, but now that the men were abroad all the mail was being collected en-masse before being sent to sorting offices in England overwhelmed with similar letters from the whole of the British Expeditionary Forces. So it was that letters began to arrive at home in bundles, where the mail had to be sorted out by the recipients into the order in which it was to be read.

Betty's first bundle contained all the letters telling her he was moving from Yorkshire to Wales and then one said that he'd got embarkation leave. Whatever that was! The last letter of her first bundle told her where he expected to be going. But the whole of that sentence was blanked out. A note in the envelope explained that for security reasons she was not allowed to receive mail containing mention of troop movements.

So she didn't know where he was; just that he was on the continent.

She asked Mrs. Blower if Walter had managed to tell her, but her letter had been censored in the same way. Betty went to see Mrs. Blower at least once a week, when she could get away. Which was getting harder now with the land work, as well as the cooking, taking more and more of her time up. She often saw Mr. Blower in the garden as now it was she who fetched any vegetables needed in the kitchen. This liberated David for work in the fields. David dreamed of going off to fight with his brother, and Mr. Blower worried about him, as he had heard tales of unscrupulous recruiting officers signing on young men, younger than David, although they were not supposed to sign men on under the age of eighteen. And David didn't even look his fifteen years. The recruiting officers were paid for every man they signed up so they had an incentive to sign up as many as they could, whatever their age.

Betty still visited her parents on her days off which were now fewer and further between. She also tried to make time to see Mrs. Cohen when she could. If she got chance she tried to let her mother know when she was coming and hope Mrs. Cohen would take the time to be at her mother's cottage, so that she could see her there. More often than not this worked.

Harvest time came, and it was a really busy time for all on the two estates. The women helped the men bring in the crops. Luckily the weather held and a good harvest was stored. It was a great boon to the war effort the newspapers said. Walter's letters were becoming more and more sporadic and much shorter. It was obvious from their tone that he was trying to keep them upbeat but some of the things he said left Betty imagining what he must have seen. Walter's birthday came and went, he was now seventeen.

Just after the harvest the weather changed and at the harvest festival in the church the choir had to sing loudly to be heard over the sound of the rain on the roof. The weather deteriorated even more into December and 1916 roared in on gales. Dancy arrived at the end of January with another black-edged telegram for one of the families in the village similar to the one he had delivered to the Grogans. Four more arrived in quick succession. Five of the twenty boys who'd left with Walter that fateful day were now casualties of the war. The war that they had been assured, when it began, would be over by Christmas.

Betty attended all the funerals. Audrey didn't. She said she hadn't known the boys but Betty knew there was a deeper reason for Audrey not to attend.

Nineteen sixteen became nineteen seventeen. Another year of hard work in the fields, and more reading and writing letters, trying to decipher what the censor had left her to read. Walter now was on a different front. He'd become good friends with one of the village boys who'd worked on the farm. Mention of the boy appeared in three of Walters letters and then he disappeared from Walter's correspondence. Betty heard that another telegram had been delivered by Dancy to one of the Major's troop's families in the village. A boy called Cyril Inman was 'missing presumed killed in action' as the war office euphemistically called it. Betty surmised that this was the unnamed boy in Walter's letters. It was at Cyril's funeral that Betty realised that Walter never named his companions. She realised, as they were singing hymns in the little church that was getting used to holding funeral services, that it was because it was so difficult to get close to someone that might not be there tomorrow. The thought made Betty shiver. That was the effect Walter's letter were beginning to have on her now.

Fourteen of the twenty still survived but then came a massive blow for the Manor. September of nineteen seventeen, another good harvest all but safely stored in the barns of both estates. The women were getting used to doing their jobs with the men and the work was therefore that little bit easier. They had two more fields to bring in and all would be ready for the winter when Mr Burton was called away from his duties to attend the Major's wife at the house. He left the foreman from the Villiers estate in charge but he never came back. Everybody worked until dark to ensure the fields would be cleared. The weather forecast was good but it was better to be safe than sorry. Make hay while the sun shines was the watchword of the harvest crew. Everyone was feeling happy that the harvest was completed when they arrived back at the farm on the hay wagon, tired but in good spirits. Turning into the yard they saw Mr. Burton standing at the stable door alone. As soon as they saw him they knew that something was wrong. Betty's first thought was that something had happened to Mrs. Burton, but then why would he be here at the stable instead of with his wife.

The women climbed down and the driver and his mate took the wagon over to the stable and began to unharness the horses. Betty watched as Mr. Burton composed himself. He coughed into his hand in order to get everyone's attention. "Leave the horses, just a minute lads. I've an important announcement to make."

They stopped what they were doing but stayed with the animals. The horses too were tired and hungry. It was very odd for Mr. Burton to stop them attending to the horses. He was generally a stickler for the welfare of all the farm's animals. "I've some very grave news from the front I'm afraid."

Betty's stomach dropped, as did a couple of the other girls whose men were away. They moved together for support, arms around each other. Betty had her hand to her mouth. "The Major has been badly injured, and his horse has been killed. They were caught in a mortar attack." He saw the girls blanched faces and realised what he had done. He continued swiftly on, in order to put their minds at rest. "He was with your men, but he was the only one injured."

The girls breathed a communal sigh of relief.

"You say the Major is injured. Is he bad?" One of the girls asked to cover their relief.

Mr. Burton swallowed. It was obviously very difficult for him to continue to talk about his good friend in this way. He took a deep breath before saying, his voice cracking under the strain of what he had to impart, "The Major has lost both legs just below the knees and his right hand." He stopped speaking. He couldn't continue.

The men with the horses began to rub them down, in order to cover Burton's obvious distress. Betty and one of the other girl's went over to him. They both put an arm on his shoulder not knowing what else to do. The man was crying. At that moment Betty felt such hatred towards the people doing this to them that she felt she could gladly have taken up a gun and shot them herself. Mr. Burton shamefacedly thanked them for their kindness and went off down the yard to check the barn, he said.

It was full dark now and the girls walked to the lane and then went their separate ways, Betty making her way back to the kitchen where Audrey had a large bowl of steaming rabbit stew ready for her. She did justice to her meal but the news from Mr. Burton certainly stopped her enjoying it. That night in her steaming hot bath she wondered where Walter was and if he'd witnessed the Major's wounding. Mr. Burton had said the Major had been with the men. She wondered if Walter could get a bath. Not if the stories in the newspapers they were now starting to receive were to be believed.

CHAPTER TEN.

The Major's wife spent an inordinate amount of time away after this news was received. During this time, as was only to be expected, she left Mr. Burton in charge. The routine that had been established over the war years, whereby the women would help during planting and harvesting, leaving the men able to manage the day to day running of the two estates between these labour intensive times, worked well. This left Mr. Burton with spare time which he spent around the stables, and when he got the opportunity, in the evenings he could be seen riding alone over the fields he'd once ridden with the Major. He became quiet and introverted over this period. The news of the Major's injuries had had a profound effect on him. He had been as gung-ho as the Major in aiding him to recruit the boys. It seemed now to everyone who knew him, that he regretted this.

The Major returned to the estate in early July. Before then Mr. Burton had planks laid over the gravel of the drive, and from the front door of the house to the lawn he had a ramp fitted. Then, planks ran along the edge of the lawn until they reached the solid lane which led to the stables.

Mr. Burton would take the Major along this path in his bath chair, most days. They would then spend most of the day around the stables, only returning to the house in the evening as dusk fell. The stable lads said they didn't talk much, they seemed comfortable in each other's company. Which wasn't what Jenny experienced inside the Manor House. She said the atmosphere almost every day could be cut with a knife. Jenny would say at tea time to Dora, Audrey and Betty that the Major's wife was always weeping, and seemed to blame the Major for going away and leaving her. She even seemed to blame him for returning injured as badly as he was. Dora had always said she didn't have a forgiving nature.

During this time, in the period before he returned home, four more of his group were injured. It was another mortar attack. Two men were maimed, one lost an arm and one was blinded. The other two were gassed, in the aftermath.

When these men returned they were like the ghosts of their former selves. They shuffled along as a group, seeking out their own company, and shunning former friends. At first there was some animosity towards them for this attitude, but people soon realised that they wanted to forget the war and all that they'd seen and done. But all anyone wanted to talk to them about was their wartime experiences, the very thing they wanted to forget.

When Betty saw them for the first time after their return she wept. She contrasted the way they were now, with the wall of faces hanging out of the army lorry, shouting and joking as they left to go to war. She sought them out in order to ask them about Walter. Did they have any news of him? Could they tell her where he was? Was he all right? But they told her exactly what they told everyone else who asked about the remaining eight men. They said, he was all right, nothing more, nothing less. They, no matter how strongly they were questioned, would not elaborate on that simple statement.

Betty didn't know the men personally. She'd seen them about and spoken to them, when she'd been out walking with Walter before the conflict, but that was all. She put their taciturnity down to this until other people told her they'd received the same answers. She knew that the maimed boys had been with Walter at the fair on the night she and Walter had met, and she was disappointed by their lack of empathy, and she said as much to Audrey one day after she'd spoken to them.

Audrey thought about Betty's complaint and at first Betty didn't think she was going to reply, but eventually she did. "I think the boys have done right by you all. They probably talked about this over there, in the trenches, amongst themselves. The questions they'd be asked and such, if any of them came home wounded. You know if anything happened to them, like it has, and they got home leaving others still there. They will all have decided what to say then. I suppose."

"Do you think so, Audrey? But why say what amounts to nothing then?"

"Look at them, Betty. Do you think your man will look any different, even if he's whole! War changes men, duck! They'll be different men that come home to those that left. There's nowt nah' surer. You can count on that."

Betty, after some thought, saw the truth in Audrey's words. She hadn't thought about it much until then. Just praying for Walter to come home safe had taken all her energy. She'd never considered the bigger picture, when he did get home. Audrey was surely right, and it was those that had stayed home that would have to accommodate the changes. Looking at the four returnees there was nothing they could do. They had been changed forever by their experiences and not only because of their injuries. Still she found herself hoping that Walter might sustain some wound, nothing too serious, just enough to bring him home to her arms again. She longed to hold him. She could manage the changes the war would have wrought just so long as he came back to her safe and well.

The Major and Mr. Burton had become a familiar sight around the estate. The Major had requested Mr. Burton have him a gun rest made by Mr. Asquith the blacksmith, which he duly did. The Major could now use his gun using the rest and most days you could hear the sound of the pair of them shooting at targets set up in the fields to the rear of the house.

"You'd think he'd have had enough of guns to last him a lifetime," Audrey said one day in the kitchen to no one in particular.

Betty had to agree. It seemed a strange hobby to take up for someone who'd been through what he had. But then there was very little he could do given his disabilities, and he'd always enjoyed outdoor pursuits.

It was around this time that Dancy delivered his next two telegrams. He was becoming something of a pariah around the village. People didn't know what sort of news he would be bringing so some had begun to shun him, expecting only the worst when he turned up. This day it was the worst. Two more of the group had been killed. That left only six of the original band still alive and fighting.

Betty attended the funerals, as she had attended all the others. The little church was full as it had been on all the other occasions. It appeared drab and lifeless now, as if it was getting used to these sad ceremonies. The Major made an appearance, wrapped in a tartan rug and with a deerstalker hat with the flaps down over his ears. He cut a sad, and dejected figure, as he sat hunched over in his wheeled chair, in sharp contrast to the man who'd ridden out and spoken to the boys, on his fine horse, before they all went away to the dreadful war.

After the service for the two boys the Major was hardly seen around the estate. Audrey told the girls at tea time that Mrs. Burton had told her that the funeral service had had a profound effect on him and he spent most of his time now in his study. He rarely called on Mr. Burton to take him out now, preferring his own company. Betty thought of the four ghosts, as she thought of the returnees, and realised what a shock it must have been for the Major to have seen them at the service. She could understand his angst after seeing them.

There was some good news in 1917; the Americans entered the fray and after some allied victories in the Middle East and Africa the already fading German morale was dealt a heavy blow. But so was village morale when just after the news about America Dancy delivered another of his telegrams. Another funeral for Betty to attend and only five of the group left now. At least she thought, Walter is one of them. The day after the service Mrs. Burton called into the kitchen to tell Audrey that the Major had summoned Mr. Burton to take him out. He was to bring the guns and the gun rest. Everyone was pleased, mostly for the Major's wife. She had lost a lot of weight and was obviously worried about him.

Betty put on the kettle and Mrs. Burton joined them, Dora, Audrey, and Jenny, who was now married to her farmhand. The wedding ceremony had been low key, because of all the funerals, Jenny hadn't wanted to parade her happiness. The ceremony had raised morale in the village though; it had given them all something positive to celebrate amid the darkness. The villagers had lined the lane back to the Manor applauding, and throwing flowers picked from the hedgerows, and Jenny had told Betty it made her feel like a princess, she'd been so proud.

Mrs. Burton and Audrey were discussing the American aspect of the war when there was noise of running inside the house. David burst into the kitchen through the house door. He was wearing wellington boots, caked with mud.

Before Audrey, or Mrs. Burton had time to chastise him, he gasped, "Call an ambulance. The Major's had an accident." And he rushed out before anyone could question him.

Mrs. Burton ran out into the hallway and did as David had bid. Everyone in the kitchen followed David's boot-prints over the chequer board, black and white tiled foyer, out of the front door to the top of the ramp. They could see men running in the direction of the stables but little else. Dora was all for following the men but the others restrained her.

"We'd only be in the way," said Jenny.

"People will want tea, when they come in. Let's get the big pot out. We'll need it no doubt," said Audrey authoritatively.

Mrs. Burton nodded to Audrey as she passed on her way back to her own apartments. Tea was duly made and Dora was allowed to push it through the house to the rear entrance, where the stable yard was, on the tea trolley. The bottom shelf had been loaded, by Jenny with large white mugs.

The ambulance arrived, closely followed by a police car. Dora served tea to all who wanted it. Though not many did. When she returned about half an hour later she was unusually quiet. Not at all her usual self. Mrs. Burton had already been with the news so Dora's story was but detail. They already knew that the Major had shot himself.

As Dora filled in the details the ambulance left. It didn't hurry, there were no bells ringing, there was no point. Later the police left after questioning Mr. Burton and the stable lads. There wasn't much they could tell them, the scene was self-explanatory.

According to what Dora had gleaned while handing out the tea, the Major had asked Mr. Burton to push him in his chair against the stable wall. From there, he explained, he could see the woods, where he used to love to ride. He then asked for a target to be set up in the middle of the field. The field had been cleared, the crop, potatoes, already stored away. The potatoes were piled at the edge of the field near the gate and covered completely in straw to stop any frost penetration. This was then covered with soil; the potatoes would be safe stored like this, until needed. The farmhands called this a potato pie, which the girls thought was funny. The men who had to bury the pie didn't think it the least bit funny. So there was no fear of anyone being injured when the target practise began. He then had Mr Burton load his gun, both barrels, which was not unusual, and set up the rifle rest that Mr. Asquith the blacksmith had made for him. There had been some discussion earlier about clay pigeon shooting but the Major wasn't agile enough for that. When the Major was satisfied everything was to his liking he asked for his second gun. This, again, wasn't unusual, as he let Mr. Burton use it, and he liked Burton to shoot with him. So Mr. Burton went off to fetch the Purdey the Major wanted. While he was away the Major wedged the loaded gun between his knees (he still had both knees with which to grip the gun). He then took the rifle rest, and reached down using his good arm, He placed the V shaped rest over the triggers. Then leaning his chin over both barrels he pressed the rest down onto the triggers and fired the gun. Unfortunately the gun slipped down as he applied pressure to the triggers and instead of the shot travelling through his head as he had wished it took away his throat leaving his head hanging by a thread of skin and flesh. He died instantly.

The police, according to Dora, had been inordinately interested in what the Major had been busy with in his study. Dora's interpretation of this was because the inspector in charge of the investigation, a man called Inman, had a son who worked occasionally on the farm. This boy had been seventeen at the time the Major formed his unit, and the boy had joined against his father's wishes. The boy had been killed. Due to the overriding patriotism at the time he didn't do anything about it, which he felt he should have done, but there were a number of the boys underage and no-one else seemed to mind, so he kept his reservations to himself. He didn't want to appear unpatriotic, especially in his line of work. Now Dora believed this was his way of getting his own back for the loss of his son.

The police took away a number of documents amongst them a letter to his solicitor. The Major's wife had protested at this but the inspector had ignored her.

"Had he left a letter for her?" asked Audrey.

Dora shrugged her shoulders. "No one mentioned her."

CHAPTER ELEVEN.

The Major's inquest coincided with news of Woodrow Wilson's fourteen point peace plan, but only Audrey saw the irony in this. Everyone else was only interested in the verdict which, as far as Audrey was concerned, was a foregone conclusion, considering his standing in the community. She was proved right. The Major was deemed to have taken his life while the balance of his mind was disturbed. The police evidence, provided from the witness box by the Inspector Dora had mentioned, contradicted this verdict, and the inspector asked for this to be noted in the transcript. According to the police the Major had spent his time in his study laboriously writing out a new will with his left hand. He had contacted his solicitor and had the will witnessed and signed in his presence. Hardly the act of a man who had lost his mind, the inspector sarcastically remarked. He had then written a letter to his wife asking her to forgive him but explaining that he felt responsible for the deaths of the young men, boys, the inspector had said, he had led off to war. He felt he'd been lied to and that in passing on these lies to people who trusted him he'd forfeited his right to live. His own severe injuries had only compounded these feelings. So he hoped for her forgiveness but he just couldn't go on. It was obvious what the inspector thought about this epistle.

The Major's wife had asked for this letter to be read out in open court and she also allowed the relevant part of the new will to be read. This ensured that the families of the twenty boys who went to war with the Major would always be allowed to live in the tied cottages they inhabited, even if they didn't work on the estate. They would always have a roof over their heads. The Major could do no more, and he thought that this was little enough, but he felt he had to do something.

This cut little ice with the inspector, but despite his protestations the verdict stood.

That was that. The inquest was over and the body was released for burial. Then came the next twist in the saga. The vicar was asked, because he had performed all the services for the fallen so far, if he would officiate at the Majors funeral, but he refused. His reason being that the Major, for whatever reasons, had taken his own life, he had therefore, died in sin. The vicar said he had to be true to himself and his beliefs, therefore he couldn't in all conscience take the service. This caused quite a stir in the village, as the Major had been a great supporter of the church. But the vicar was adamant. Eventually the chaplain from the Major's regiment took the service at the Manor and the Major's remains were interred in the family crypt on the estate, so the local church wasn't involved in the service in any way.

There was some dissent in the village. Mutterings about there being some remains to bury in the crypt, there was some support for the vicar, and for the police, but at the end of the day the whole village turned out to honour the man. The Major had been highly thought of, and everyone agreed that he had been misled himself. Most people said he would be sadly missed. Betty noticed the 'ghosts' stayed long after most of the mourners had left. They stood arms linked and silent as if no one else was there.

She would go and sit on the bench by the dovecote alone, and talk to Walter about the events of the day when anything out of the ordinary had occurred. This way she felt closer to him in their own special place. That was how she noticed the four men. When she left the bench, to go back to the kitchen they were still there, standing silently, grouped around the entrance to the crypt, keeping vigil as dusk fell. Above their heads as evening drew in the doves flew home to roost.

1917 became 1918 four years into a war that was supposed to be over by Christmas. The war to end wars!

After the inquest the Major's wife stayed on just long enough to oversee the shutting down of the Manor. She arranged for all the staff to gather in the foyer, where she explained, close to tears, that the place held too many memories for her and that she was going to stay in London for a while. This was only to be a temporary break until she felt able to come back. She left Mr. Burton in charge with orders to organise the staff as he felt fit. She thanked them all for their kindness, good wishes and for their hard work during difficult times. With that she left. The solicitor drove her to the station in his motorcar. Betty would never see her again.

When she'd gone Audrey and Betty walked back to the kitchen through the dust sheeted rooms, darkened by the closed shutters. More ghosts, thought Betty as she remembered the nights when she and Audrey had prepared food for the hundreds of people entertained over the years by the Major and his wife. Albert and Lily left also. Albert explained to Mr. Burton that he couldn't stay on without the Major as the place could never be the same. Dora remarked that with the Major gone he'd have to do some proper work under Mr. Burton, and everyone agreed. Though no one told her so. Lily left to be with her husband. She was a quiet woman and Betty had never got to know her well, at all. She always did her work but never mixed with the other staff unless she had to. She was a loner. There was no call now, with the Major and his wife both gone, for an upstairs maid. Mr. Burton had offered her other work, as she was a conscientious person, and did her work well, but she declined.

So the year progressed. March and the planting season arrived. With less need for the kitchen even Audrey helped out in the fields. Food was prepared for the workers, casual and staff. This was served outdoors as it was a glorious summer. When she wasn't in the kitchen, which was more often than not, now that there were no banquets to prepare, Betty helped Walter's father in the garden.

She enjoyed working in the glasshouses and she would listen to him talk about Walter. Tales about how he fell in the duck pond and nearly drowned when he was seven, and how the rest of that year was spent teaching Walter and David to swim. Albert was already working then. There were many stories; some she felt sure were very private memories for Walter's father but which he wished to share with her, just so he could talk about his son. Over the summer months she felt a deep bond growing between them. She looked upon Walter's father as a friend and she trusted him with her dreams. The dreams she and Walter shared about their life together when he came home and they married. She even told him about the dovecote and the bench and her conversations with Walter there. He would only nod at these times, he said very little. He was a very quiet, inward looking man. Deep, her mother would have called him. She occasionally thought she saw tears in his eyes at these moments, but she could never be sure.

More and more times the newspapers were using words like 'Truce' and 'Armistice'. Headlines splashed across the front pages of all the newspapers talked of peace. Audrey had taken to having a paper delivered now that the Major's wife had gone and Dora couldn't purloin the house newspaper.

Harvest time arrived and peace was all the talk in the fields. The Germans were beaten, but they would not give in.

Some of the Villiers's people that they worked with had mentioned half of the men who went with the captain had been killed. The captain himself was missing, so both estates had suffered greatly and Audrey said that would be the way all across the land. Yet their foe would keep on fighting. Sometimes Audrey's despair was almost tangible, it was almost as if Audrey carried the weight of all the horrors that had happened on her own shoulders. Betty felt for her. She was a loving and caring woman, Betty felt honoured to be her friend.

Everyone was exasperated with the politicians. Men were still dying, yet all they did was talk, arguing over trivialities. At times it was too much for Betty to bear. It was a month since any post had arrived from the front. The families of the five remaining survivors of the Major's band were desperate for news. All the talk was of the war ending yet they still had loved ones in danger. Surely someone somewhere could end this travesty. Someone must have the power to call a halt to this senseless killing.

November began cold and frosty. Still no word from the front. More talk of Armistice but by now people were sick of the talk; it was action that was required. Suddenly as if by magic on the ninth of November, Kaiser Wilhelm II went into exile and then abdicated. The newspapers said no one knew where he'd fled to. The best guess was Holland. November ninth, Armistice talks officially began between the allies and Germany, although talk in the newspapers was still guarded. With this news a cautious optimism spread throughout the village. The end was almost in sight, Betty felt like she could touch it.

Then Dancy arrived with the telegrams. Betty saw him from the bench as he rode past the gate to the Manor. She ran as fast as she could through the garden calling to Walter's father but not stopping. She careered out through the gate and down the lane to the cottages. She passed the gypsy woman without a glance, in her desperate dash. She saw Dancy as he rode away, and heard the anguished cry from Walter's mother, before she saw her on her knees, head on the path, in front of the cottage door, the black edged telegram unopened, laying on the stone flags in front of her. Betty stopped momentarily, when she saw the dreaded envelope, but she walked along the path and knelt down putting her arms around her, now, never to be, mother-in-law. The two women sobbed together, on their knees uncontrollably.

"This is not right. Don't believe this."

The voice penetrated their grief. Betty looked up the tears streaming down her face. The gypsy woman, her figure distorted by the tears, held the telegram, still unopened in her hand, "This is not right. You'll see the boy again when the roses bloom. Mark my words." She said. She handed the telegram to Walter's mother, and just as Walter's father arrived she turned and walked away, closing the little white, wooden gate, which Walter had made, behind her. "Mark my words, when the roses bloom," she called back over her shoulder. Then she was gone.

Walter's father opened the envelope and read the words printed there. He sat on the bench below the window the paper hanging loosely from his work, worn hands. Tears ran down his weather beaten, cheeks soundlessly, and the paper dropped, unnoticed from his fingers. The three of them cried, as the sky darkened around them, and the first snow of winter began to fall unnoticed on the village. Dancy had delivered five telegrams, all bearing the same message. Missing in action. Presumed killed.

Dancy delivered his telegrams on the ninth of November, by a cruel twist of fate the politicians delivered peace on the eleventh of November not that anyone in the benighted village noticed. Of the twenty boys who left with the Major only four survived and they were ghosts of their former selves. They drifted around the village either together or in pairs, never alone, one always leading the blinded man by his arm. A sad reminder to everyone who saw them of what had happened in The War To End Wars.

Slowly, as the village prepared for yet another multiple funeral service, it began to sink into the collective consciousness that the war was finally over. The village had paid a terrible price. Around them other villages and towns were preparing celebrations, but the village's own celebration preparations were muted in deference to those who'd been lost. Everyone was relieved that this terrible war was at last over but the Manor itself was sunk in despair.

After the service, which Betty sleep-walked through, she continued to work at the house, but it was not now, and could never be again, the same. All her dreams had died in some foreign land. She didn't even know where, or how. Her life could never be the same. She sat and talked to Walter at the dovecote many times in the next few weeks. But sometimes when she made her way to it she found Walter's father there. At these times she slipped quietly away, not wishing to disturb him, knowing what he was doing. Walter's loss had aged him, and he stooped now as he worked tirelessly in the garden, growing vegetables that were no longer needed at the Manor House any longer. Walter's mother on the other hand grasped the gypsy's words tightly to her heart. Betty didn't think at the time, that she'd heard what the gypsy woman had said, but she had, and now she would nod, knowingly when people offered their condolences, and would tell anyone who would listen about the prophecy. People began to shun her thinking the loss had affected her brain. She planted two rose trees in the front garden of the cottage and over the coming years would tend them lovingly. Nothing would ever dent her belief that one day Walter would return.

CHAPTER TWELVE.

Betty spent more time now with her mother and father. The loss of Walter had made her realise that she'd been neglecting the two people she loved most in the world, and that they were not young any more. While with her mother she'd rekindled her friendship with Mrs. Cohen, and she decided now was a good time to leave the Manor. It had been in her mind for some time, since the Major's wife left, but her ties there were strong and she felt a kinship with Audrey, in particular, but she knew she must leave; as the Major's wife had said, too many memories. Mrs. Cohen had offered her some work on the stall at the fairground, and she knew this would give her some breathing space until she could find somewhere permanent. This work had been the deciding factor in making up her mind to leave.

It was with a heavy heart that she told Mrs. Burton that she was leaving. Mr. Burton did his level best to persuade her to change her mind, but Mrs. Burton realised that it was not the job she didn't want, but the memories. When the day finally arrived it was a tearful teatime in the Manor House kitchen. Mr. and Mrs. Burton called in for a little while, and Mr. Burton promised her work if she ever wanted to come back. When the Burtons left, the old team of Dora, Jenny and Audrey remained. At first nothing really was said. Enforced jocularity being the order of the day, strangely enough it was Dora who first broke down and then the floodgates opened and the four friends stood together before the great range, as if it were some kind of sacrificial altar, and Betty was the sacrifice, hugging each other and weeping floods of tears. Slowly composure returned and a little shamefacedly Dora kissed Betty on the cheek and left the room, blowing her nose into an off-white man's handkerchief, after wishing her well.

Next it was Jenny's turn, and with more tears she told her nct to forget her friends and to keep in touch. She made her promise to visit regularly, and at her cottage; this caused Betty a little shudder, unnoticed by her friend, as she remembered the plans she and Walter had had for the same cottage.

When Jenny left, it was Audrey and Betty alone, they hugged for the longest time saying nothing. Betty breathed in the smell of flour and cooking which always, in the years to come, would remind her of Audrey and this particular moment in time. Audrey was the first to release the hug. The cook stood before her with a hand on each of Betty's shoulders, "I don't need to tell you what we all think of you do I?"

Betty found she couldn't speak. Now that finally the time had come, all of her carefully prepared words had left her. She was emotionally drained. Speechless. So she shook her head, tears welling in her eyes. Audrey took her in her arms again, "You know I love you like a daughter. More than a daughter. So get yourself off now and don't forget where I am."

With those words Audrey left the room and Betty was alone in the kitchen where she'd spent so many happy hours. She left the room by the familiar door and followed the well-worn path to the lane and home to her parents, weeping all the way, a mixture of sadness and joy. She'd intended to visit Walter's parents but she knew she couldn't in the state she was in. So she wept her way home, arriving with red-rimmed eyes and a soaking handkerchief, to the comforting arms of her mother who sat her down in the kitchen, and kindly made her a cup of tea, leaving her alone with it, to quietly settle down, before returning to talk of mundane matters pertaining to the house, and her bedroom, when she felt better.

Betty's mother never mentioned the episode again for which Betty was always grateful. Leaving the Manor was one of the hardest things she ever had to do. She never thought she would ever find friendship like that again.

Betty helped her mother out at Mrs. Cohen's, and travelled to the fairs with her in her motorcar. The memories evoked by the war were still there for everyone, but with the end of the war people wanted to enjoy themselves and so the fairs were always very busy. There seemed to Betty, a manic kind of jollity around, people seemed overly happy. It appeared to be a kind of forced happiness; Betty found it strange but it made the stalls busy and kept her mind from wandering to darker thoughts. The coconut shy and the jewellery stalls were popular attractions and always did good business. Among the crowds, Betty noticed the maimed and scarred veterans, the men who ducked at the loud noises and who didn't like the flashing lights. She saw them as they tried to enjoy themselves with their friends, but she noticed they seemed better when they were with others who'd been to war, just like the ghosts on the estate, she thought. Although Mrs. Cohen did her best to find Betty work there was never enough to go round, and after her job at the Manor Betty found herself getting bored waiting for Mrs. Cohen to tell her when she had work for her. So it was that Betty decided to try for a job at the local laundry one day, after talking to a girl she met while on the coconut shy. The girl, who she remembered from school, had a job there and she said the money was good and the girls companionable. Betty thought that the laundry couldn't be more different to the Manor, which was what she wanted, so she applied at the office, quoting the girl's name as reference, as the girl had told her to, and she was surprised to be taken on immediately. She was under no illusion that the work would be hard, and the girl had told her that the work was hot, which it proved to be. Betty was used to hard work though and soon got into the swing of it. It was entirely different to what she'd been used to, and the girls, although friendly enough, with one or two exceptions, were not like her friends at the Manor. The work was noisy, hot, monotonous and regimented, and so there was no time to develop the camaraderie that she'd had at the Manor but that suited Betty. She buried herself in her work and just got on with the job.

Betty found she had a problem with one of the older women she worked with. The woman, whose name was Joan Lowes, Joan to her friends, had been dismissed from the Manor by Mrs. Burton, and she knew Betty's mother was friendly with her, so at every opportunity she made some remark about Betty to her workmates.

Remarks such as, "How are the mighty fallen." And "Isn't the laundry getting posh all of a sudden."

Betty ignored her and kept out of her way, but she was a vindictive personality, and Betty felt that one day there would be a confrontation. For the most part the other workers were too busy to take much notice of what Joan said, but Betty was afraid that she would lose her job if Joan kept pushing her and she retaliated. Betty had always been quiet, and she found herself surprised at her attitude towards this woman. Betty knew that under normal circumstances she would probably have been in floods of tears, she'd always been that way, a consequence of being spoiled as a child she thought. But since losing Walter and, all the funerals she'd attended she'd found herself toughening up. All she wanted to do to Joan Lowes, when she started with the snide remarks, was hit her. This was very unlike her, and she didn't like the feeling it gave her, but she knew, in the laundry environment that she must not show any weakness or her life there would quickly become unbearable. She remembered Jenny and Dora, at the Manor, and Dora had liked Jenny, but she still had had her in tears more than once with her practical jokes, and her gossip. Betty wasn't going to let that happen to her.

Luckily for Betty one of the supervisors noticed what was going on and, not wanting to lose two good workers, moved Betty to the pressing department. This proved to be a godsend for Betty who found she loved the work and quickly picked up the intricacies of the pressing machines. She soon found herself one of the top pressers, pressing ever more awkward clothing and earning better money because of it. This news soon reached the ears of Joan Lowes, who complained bitterly to the supervisor who'd moved Betty. But as the woman said to Joan, "You had the opportunity to move and didn't want to leave your friends. You can't now complain that the girl who took the job is doing well at it. Oh! And by the way, she wouldn't have been moved in the first place if you hadn't been picking on her." This frustrated Joan even more, but she knew better than to argue with this particular supervisor and so, in the end she kept quiet and Betty wasn't troubled with her again.

The work in the pressing room was hard, and hot. But as Betty enjoyed it, and enjoyed the money even more, she just got on with it. The hours were regular, not like at the Manor, where fourteen hour days had been normal when dinner parties were to be cooked for. The hours suited Betty because it meant she could still go out to the fairs with Mrs. Cohen. She found her work at the laundry simple, now she knew how to use the machines. The job wasn't that hard, so a couple of late nights with Mrs. Cohen didn't represent any hardship for her. Life was now, two years after the war to end wars, beginning to look good again. It was not the same; that could never be, but it was better than she thought it ever could be, at the time. Then one day at the Goose Fair, she met Mathew, and life got even better.

As with Walter, it was Mrs. Cohen who noticed him first. He and three other men walked past the coconut shy and jewellery stall, pushing racing bicycles by the seats. Expertly manoeuvring them through the crowds, without using the handlebars. Mrs. Cohen, nodded towards the group and pulled a, get them, sort of face, which caused Betty to laugh. The four men made their way towards the boxing booth, and were soon lost in the milling crowds, but a couple of hours later they re-appeared, looking battered and bruised but definitely in high spirits.

"Let's go on the coconuts," said a tall, blond, balding man pushing a red Raleigh.

They all ambled over and Naomi, not to miss a trick, pushed her way through the gate between the stalls and grabbed a bucket of wooden balls used to throw at the coconuts, from beneath the counter and said, "Come on you big fine lads should have no problem knocking these off." She began to hand over the balls to the men, who laughing at her effrontery, leaned their bicycles against the side of the stall where Betty was standing. The last man to lean his bicycle up, took his missiles from Betty and said sheepishly, "Thanks."

The balding man was already throwing. "Roll up! Roll up! Watch these strapping lads win a coconut," called Naomi to the passing throng.

"Is she always like that?" asked the man she'd just served.

Betty nodded. "Mostly."

He threw his balls and missed. Never getting close. His friends were collecting more so he said, "Looks like we're going again." He grinned. "I'm Matty, by the way."

His lip was cut, and started to bleed as he smiled. He grimaced and wiped away the blood with the back of his hand. He threw again, this time he hit his target but it only wobbled in the cup. He took a handkerchief from his jacket pocket and wiped his lip properly.

"Not much good at this am I?" He grinned again, and bled again.

"What have you been up to?"

"We've been in the boxing booth. Harry won."

A stocky man with a shock of black hair nodded towards her as he launched a ball which knocked a coconut over in its sawdust socket but didn't unseat it.

"He won?" asked Betty incredulous, looking at the battle scarred man. He looked in worse shape than Matty.

They all four looked at each other and laughed. By now, thanks to Naomi's calling, they'd drawn quite a crowd, and more people were asking for balls. Betty and Naomi were busy handing them out when the four young men got their bikes and began to walk away into the darkening night. "Betty," she called after Matty's receding back. He turned and looked quizzically towards her.

"My name. It's Betty."

He nodded, waved, and disappeared into the colourful melee following his friends. She watched until she couldn't distinguish him any more, among the moving, ever changing mass.

"Mmm," said Naomi, smiling.

Betty blushed and said nothing.

The following day, a Saturday, Matty came back, this time alone. Now he had a black eye and his lip was purple and swollen. He apologised for his appearance and he hung about the stall until Naomi set him on making the tea for the three of them. "You'll have to muck in if you're going to hang around here; today's a busy day," she chided Matty who laughed and mucked in, taking it all in good part.

Before the stalls got really busy the two women had learned that Matty was a coal miner who worked with his three companions at a nearby colliery. They enjoyed keeping fit and in their spare time, what little they had, they sparred with each other and trained using home-made punch bags and other home-made equipment. Usually between the four of them they could defeat the fairground boxer. They then shared the prize money. It was a great boost to their meagre wages.

They visited all the fairs they could cycle to when work allowed. Three of them would wear the fairground boxer down but get beat, and then the fourth would last the distance, and so collect the prize, at least that was the plan; usually it worked. Sometimes they had to argue for their money but generally, even given in bad grace, they got paid.

As the stalls became busier Matty asked if he could see Betty again before leaving. She agreed to meet him later in the week, and over the next few weeks, Matty would cycle over and take Betty out whenever time and work would allow. So it was that the courtship began.

Betty thought it only fair to tell Matty about Walter as soon as she realised that the relationship was getting serious. Matty said he understood but he gave her to understand that he wasn't Walter and could never be him. He would wait, give her time, but he could only ever be himself and if she couldn't accept that she should let him know now rather than keeping both of them hanging on.

Betty appreciated all that Matty had said. She realised he was a very different person to Walter; the courtship continued. Tentatively at first, but as time passed their feelings grew. Betty introduced him to her parents and they got on well, which pleased her. Matty got on especially well with her dad.

She plucked up courage after a couple of months, and finally took the walk with him that led to the Manor where she introduced him to Audrey and Dora. Over cups of tea and cakes (Audrey had been baking) Matty won over her two good friends. Especially Dora. Audrey just nodded and squeezed her hand as she left, but that nod meant everything to Betty. Audrey approved. It was at this meeting that she found out Jenny was away from work because she was pregnant. Betty had been so busy that she'd neglected her friends at the Manor. She realised as they walked back down the lane towards her mother's cottage, that this was the first time she'd been to the Manor this year. This saddened her and she made a promise to herself that she would make more effort to keep in touch with these people, her very good friends. Even as they walked home she realised that they weren't visiting Jenny because Matty had to leave soon, as he was working early in the morning. So much for her resolution.

She had though, introduced Matty to Walter's father, something she'd been dreading. They'd shook hands and the meeting had been a little strained at first, which was only to be expected, Matty had said afterwards. But Walter's father had said that Matty was a lucky man, and that Betty was like a daughter to him, he hoped that they would be very happy together. It was an emotional time for him but he managed the meeting very well. Betty could see how much it affected him, and she squeezed his hand as he kissed her cheek. He just nodded in return. They'd met, as they were leaving, walking down the path to the lane; Betty had seen Mr. Blower pottering in the garden. Betty had explained that they intended to go to the cottage but were pleased to see him there. He nodded his understanding, and had said it was probably better not to go to the cottage, as seeing Betty with someone else would only upset Mrs. Blower. Matty said nothing. As they took there leave of Mr. Blower, Betty thought how he seemed to have shrunk, from the big man he used to be. He now looked like a little old man. Walter's loss and Mrs. Blower's attitude to it had taken their toll on him.

On the walk home Betty told Matty about the gypsy and her prophesy and how it had affected Mrs. Blower. Matty had shrugged and told her how he'd seen grief affect people in different ways.

Sometimes it was the only way people could come to terms with such a great loss he'd said. Betty asked him to explain. Matty said sometimes a loss is so great that the only way people can cope is by refusing to believe it. By finding some way to circumvent the truth. In Mrs. Blower's case the gypsy gave her the perfect escape route. So now, even though deep down she knows Walter is dead, the gypsy's prophecy allows her to carry some hope that one day he'll come back. It's just a way of allowing her to carry on, otherwise she'd probably lose her mind completely. Walter meant that much to her.

Betty asked when Matty had seen such grief, expecting him to tell her about someone he knew who'd been lost in the war. "It's nothing to talk about. Sometimes it happens." He shrugged again. Betty was beginning to see with Matty that the shrug of the shoulders was his way of closing a conversation. She knew now this was a subject he didn't want to talk about. She could also see from what he'd just said that he thought deeply about things. They finished the walk back to the cottage and Matty's bicycle, in silence. They arranged to meet again at the weekend, and Matty rode off, after calling goodbye to her parents, waving as he went. A deep one, Betty thought. You've got another deep one. She smiled as she opened the door and heard the kettle singing promising a nice hot cup of tea.

In September of 1921 they were married. The wedding took place at the village church, scene of so many sad occasions over the last few years. Audrey insisted on doing the catering, even supplying a two tier wedding cake. The wedding breakfast took place in the village hall, and the celebrations continued on into the night. Everyone was welcome, even Betty's ghosts made an appearance, albeit briefly. The four came as one, and wished them both well, all of them shaking hands with the happy couple. Guests of honour though were Matty's parents, who had made the journey down from Tyneside for the happy day. It was the first time both sets of parents had met, although Betty had made the journey twice, when they had been courting, Matty's parents had never made the opposite journey. So it was a double celebration and everyone seemed to get on really well and the day was a great success. One sad note on the day was when Betty noticed Walter's father standing at the wall near the church hall gate, he raised his hand in acknowledgement, and Betty waved back. Walter's parents had been invited to the wedding but declined. Mr. Blower had said his wife wasn't up to the excitement and Betty had accepted the explanation, but both of them knew the real reason. Mr. Blower had said he would try to get to the church to see her, and he'd kept his promise. Which meant a lot to Betty on her special day.

Before the couple left the festivities Betty had time for a few moments with her old companions from the Manor. They all wished her well, Jenny with her baby, and Audrey reminded the new couple not to be strangers. A few tears were shed, but these were tears of happiness. And so Betty and Matty left their guests celebrating and set off with Mr. Burton driving the little trap to the station where they caught a train to a new life together.

CHAPTER THIRTEEN.

Matty had secured a company house at the colliery where he worked as a coal hewer spending long hours at the coal face. He worked shifts and had to be at work on Monday morning at five a.m. after the Saturday of his wedding. A honeymoon was out of the question. Betty had already handed in her notice at the laundry as travelling to her job was not possible. So it was that she became a miner's wife. For the first time in her life she had her own home. She thought fondly, of the times she'd looked through the cottage windows with Walter on the Manor, and of the plans she'd made; now she had a chance to make at least some of her dreams come true. Her training at the Manor under Audrey was now to stand her in good stead.

On Monday morning, after seeing her new husband off to work she stood before the grubby, black lead range in her sparsely furnished kitchen; all the furniture had been donated by well-wishers, even the marital bed. She went to the back door of her two-up, two-down terraced cottage, almost identical to her mother's, now so far away; she looked out of the ill-fitting door at the shared yard. Everywhere she looked was covered in a thin film of coal dust. The air was thick and even tasted and smelled of it. She saw the rusting tin bath hanging from a nail knocked into the outside toilet wall. She would have to carry that in before, five in the evening, and make sure there was enough hot water for her husband to have a bath after his shift. He'd told her that he would probably have to work twelve hours to get his quota in. He explained that he was paid by piece work, therefore to earn a wage he had to cut a certain amount of coal. The seam he was working was a bad seam and so it took the gang he worked with longer to fill their quota. He hoped soon to be moving to a better seam, but that was in the future; now he just had to grin and bear it. Thinking about the bath she realised that she'd never seen a miner after his shift. Matty had said he would be dirty, but how dirty? Dirty like her father when he came home from the forest. She shook her head. She knew she had a lot to learn, but for now, she could begin with something she did know about, the range. She cleaned out the flues and black leaded it before lighting the fire, and, heading off to the company shops for provisions.

The company owned everything around the village, Matty had explained, so all the money Matty earned, one way or another went back to the pit company; they didn't like to think of the miners spending money elsewhere, so they made sure that their shops were the nearest. She'd made a list of things she'd need and intended using her final week's wages from the laundry to provide Matty's tea tonight. She'd often gone shopping with her mother, but this was a new experience, she'd never been shopping for herself. Before at the Manor, everything had been in the cupboards, or outside in the stores, or freshly picked on the vegetable table, even down to the eggs she would have to buy now. At the Manor Walter would have supplied them, she swallowed down the lump in her throat as again her thoughts strayed to her life before. This was her choice now, she must get on with it. She dismissed her earlier thoughts as homesickness and walked on in the direction of the shops through the grubby, dirty streets. The red brick, cottages loomed over her as she walked down the cobbled lane, some of them without even glass in the windows. Hessian sacks blowing in the wooden frames. She knew Walter would always be with her. She thought back, as she walked, to the day before her wedding, when for the last time as a single woman she'd visited the dovecote and sitting on the bench, said goodbye forever to Walter. She wiped away a tear as she entered the greengrocer's shop. She looked at the sorry wares on offer and thought back to the fresh vegetables she was used to using. She picked over what was there and managed to purchase some overpriced carrots, a parsnip and a swede. Not knowing exactly what time Matty would be home made a stew the order of the day. She completed her purchases with a few potatoes, and headed to the butchers where she bought a scrawny chicken carcase and turned her face homewards.

On her journey back from her first shopping expedition Betty met and spoke to some of her neighbours. She found herself to be something of a celebrity. Everyone seemed to know who she was. It was obvious word had got round about Matty Campbell's new wife, and the village was out to see her, but discreetly. Miners generally married from among their own community. The life being so hard, the women needed to be tough enough, and understanding enough of the miner's way of life, to be able to cope. It wasn't easy being a miner's wife. Betty found her neighbours wary of her, as is often the case with strangers in a close community, but willing to give her a chance. She knew after her first meeting with them that it would take time to be able to call any of them friends.

When she arrived back at her cottage Betty, using flour she'd brought with her from her mother's, baked some bread, enough to last until Wednesday, just as she had at the Manor. She then made a stew and dumplings, using the last of her flour. Now after the bread making she had an idea of the speed of her oven. She knew when to put the stew in so that it would be piping hot, and the chicken would be properly cooked, for her husband coming in from work. She filled the water tank, and altered the flues to make sure the water would be hot, angling the flames under the rear boiler. Now, finally she put on the kettle. There was no hanger as there was on the range at the Manor; here she had a moveable plate on which to stand the kettle and which swung over the coals. She did this and soon the kettle was singing away. While it boiled she went outside to the shed at the bottom of the communal yard, next to the chemical toilet. This was the fuel store. In here she found some coal and a supply of logs. Matty had told her that the women went onto the pit tips, where the waste from the mine was dumped, and sorted through this to find fuel for their own fires. They would also bring home any wood they found and the men cut this up for logs. Matty had made sure there was a plentiful supply of fuel for Betty, until she learned her way around from the other women. It was while she was filling her bucket with coal, using a ball pein hammer that Matty had hung on the back of the fuel store door to break up the larger lumps, that Betty met her next door neighbour.

"Can I borrow your hammer, duck? I wish that lazy bugger of mine would hang one on the door like yours has. Mine'd never think on't. He never fills the coal y'see. He wouldn't know where to start. Burning a hole through't shaft to thread string'd be too much for 'im. He's useless that one a' mine."

Betty handed over the tool, aghast and amazed at the way this creature talked about her husband. She'd never heard the like before. The woman proceeded to break up the lumps into more manageable pieces, which she loaded into her bucket. She was a stooped, grey haired woman with a Robin cigarette dangling from her lips which had stained the front of her hair yellow with nicotine. Her hair, which was supposed to be in a bun, had escaped and was now hanging in, lank locks across her face as she worked. Betty watched with interest as the woman threw some of the broken pieces onto a pile near the side of the shed. The woman noticed her watching. "That's bat love. See how it's grey and doesn't shine."

Betty nodded. "Don't put that on your fire, it'll explode when it gets hot. It's dangerous. It's caused house fires afore now. You're not from round here are you?"

Betty was still looking at the 'bat', as her neighbour called it, and checking her own bucket.

"No," answered Betty, throwing pieces of 'bat' away as she spoke. "My dad works in the forest. We burned logs."

"You'll soon get the hang of it. You've got a good man, Matt Campbell, he's a good 'un. Not a drinker like mine, useless bugger."

Betty was taken aback she'd never heard a woman swear before, even in the laundry.

"Annie Clegg." The woman wiped a grimy hand on a well washed, but grubby, wrap around pinafore that had once sported a floral pattern, and offered it to Betty.

"Betty... " she had to think, "Betty Campbell."

Annie Clegg laughed, never losing her cigarette, much to Betty's astonishment, showing more gaps than brown, stained teeth. "You'll soon get used to that too." She handed back the hammer and shuffled off up the yard without a backward glance, carrying her laden bucket in two hands in front of her. "When we go gleaning, I'll give you a shout," Annie said without turning around or waiting for a reply.

Betty hung the hammer back on its nail and then sifted through her bucket again, removing more of the 'bat'. She wondered about what Annie had said and thought she must remember to ask Matty what 'gleaning' was.

She filled her bucket anew making sure it was coal she put into it this time. She found that the best way to carry it, when it was full was as she'd seen Annie do it. Once indoors she spooned tea into the waiting pot after first warming it with steaming water from the singing kettle. Once the tea was made and had brewed she sat down in one of the two, hard, spindle backed chairs in the kitchen and poured herself a cup, which she enjoyed immensely. Sitting in front of her own fire, waiting her husband's return from work. It was the first time she'd sat down all day. She felt satisfied and very proud and not a little weary.

The rest of her day went by without incident. When Matty got home, after a twelve hour shift, she had plenty of hot water ready, and he needed it. She'd never seen anyone so dirty, black from head to toe. She did enjoy washing his back though, she had to admit to herself, smiling conspiratorially. Her stew was a great success, and she'd made enough to warm up for the following day, this time with bread instead of dumplings. The chicken carcase was simmering nicely over the stove. She intended making that into a warming soup, a recipe that Audrey had taught her. Audrey wasted nothing; she always used the bones of anything she cooked to make soups. Betty intended to do the same. Waste not want not was going to be her motto, she'd decided, after seeing the state of the veg in the greengrocer's and realising the prices asked were the norm.

As the pair sat contentedly in front of the range that night after dinner, Betty told Matty about her meeting with Annie Clegg and of learning about 'bat'. Matty laughed and apologised for not warning her. He said it had never crossed his mind that someone wouldn't know what 'bat' was. Betty then asked about gleaning, and Matty explained that was what the women called hunting coal out from the waste tip. It was a good sign he said that Annie was going to call for her when they went next. It showed that Annie had accepted her. Betty did the pots then and they retired for the night, both dog tired, they slept the sleep of the just in each other's arms.

Betty was a person of habit and soon she had her life working to a routine, baking bread twice a week, shopping as little as possible and cooking meals that would last two days or could be used as leftovers for stews and soups. She soon grew to realise how much she owed Audrey for the lessons she'd learned, without realising she was being taught anything about running a home. Particularly about cooking. She had got so used to cooking, large, almost industrial amounts of food and bread at the Manor that she found it difficult at first to cook the small amounts needed for just the two of them.

It was on one of her bread making days that she got the idea that was to help integrate her into the community. When she'd been gleaning coal with the others, Annie had told her how much she hated baking bread, and wondered if she could possibly buy a loaf from Betty, when she baked hers. Betty had already told Annie about her work at the Manor and about how much bread they had used there. Betty had agreed and sold Annie a loaf. On thinking over what Annie had said Betty wondered if Annie would like Betty to make her bread for her. Betty enjoyed baking and she thought if Annie bought the flour and yeast and gave her coal for the range it would relieve Annie of a job she disliked and help Betty's fuel store, as she disliked gleaning coal. When Betty put the idea to Annie, she jumped at the chance of someone else doing the baking for her. They agreed a price of two buckets of coal for three loaves and the deal was made. Once Annie spread the word Betty was soon baking bread for quite a few of the women in the locality. The deal worked well for Betty too. She ended up not having to pay for her own bread as her customers always brought more yeast and flour than was needed for their orders. Betty ended up with a full fuel store and free bread into the bargain!

The women would gather early at Betty's house on baking days and spend the time waiting for their orders, gossiping. Some of them were even bringing tea which they made and shared among the customers. It was a far cry from when Betty first started baking for them. Then they would come and collect their bread, confirm their order for the next time and leave. Now some of them were at the door before the first dough entered the oven. Betty didn't mind it was at these times that she learned a lot about the way these mining women thought and lived. About the fears they had for their men. She'd never thought too much about the work Matty did and he never talked about his job. Listening to these women gave her an insight into just how dangerous the work was, and at what cost the coal she burned in her grate came. Even her own father, it turned out, had a hand in the mining industry. Some of the timber he dragged from the forest found its way down the pits as props, and wedges and chocks. Listening to these women made her more afraid for her husband with every conversation.

Betty was now managing to save the little money from her baking to bolster Matty's paltry wage. But even as she began to do this the mine owners cut the rate they were paying the men and her hard-earned savings soon disappeared.

CHAPTER FOURTEEN.

The kitchen was full at Betty's as was now normal on baking days. The women had been talking about one thing and another, when one of the women, a newcomer to the group, but known to some of the others, mentioned a man by name. The room went quiet as the woman began to talk of this man and his affair with another miner's wife. Annie Clegg, who'd been sitting quietly by the fire smoking, interrupted the woman, mid-sentence saying, "A slice of a cut loaf's never missed Dotty. You've to remember that. Such talk as this could cause trouble. An' we don't want that underground. Do we?"

The woman looked sheepishly around the room and taking the next loaves ready, bid her farewells and left. "Don't like that sort of talk, Betty," Annie said, more to the remaining women than to Betty herself. "Can't have trouble caused by gossip spread by silly women who should know better. Men's got a hard enough job without worrying about who's talking about their wives. Talk's cheap."

There was a muttering of agreement among the gathered women, and the subject was never broached again, not in Annie's hearing anyway.

Betty was removing the next loaves from the oven; the atmosphere was still a little subdued after Dotty's early departure when Annie said, leaning towards Betty, "How far gone are ye'."

Betty looked askance.

Annie nodded to her stomach and winked. "Been feelin' sick of a mornin'."

Betty realised that the others were listening intently to their conversation. She still didn't understand what Annie was talking about.

"We're all friends ere'." Annie waved her arm expansively around, including everyone in the tiny room. "I've delivered all of their young 'uns at one time or another."

The congregation all nodded to one another and laughed. Finally the penny dropped and Betty nearly dropped her loaves. She had been feeling a little queasy in the mornings for a few weeks now and tired in the afternoons but she'd never even thought she could be pregnant.

"Nearly four month's I'd say," nodded Annie knowingly looking in the general direction of Betty's stomach. They all laughed, Betty most of all. She couldn't wait for Matty to get home so that she could tell him. Now she had some real news to write to her mother and her friends at the Manor about. She surreptitiously patted her belly.

Just as she was doing this there was a knock at the door and the last of her Tuesday customers entered the room. She looked flushed and was out of breath as if she'd been running.

"Dave's just come in," she began without preamble. "He says there's been a big fall at Harworth. Some men's lost." The atmosphere in the tiny kitchen changed immediately. From one of joyous merriment to one of despair, in seconds. Every woman in the room was now with the women of Harworth. There but for the grace of god, and each one felt it. Every woman there knew what those women far away were feeling. They had all, at one time or another, been in a situation where they were waiting for their own men to come home, and dreading the knock on the door, except Betty. Sitting watching the bath water get cold in front of the fire. Silence permeated the room, each with their own thoughts, until Annie, almost to herself, began to recite the Lord's Prayer, and one by one the others joined in. There was nothing else they could think of to do to show their solidarity. It made for a sombre meeting after that, each one taking their bread as it was baked and leaving with just a nodded goodbye.

When the room was empty and Betty began clearing away and tidying her kitchen her mind wandered back to the moment Sadie Johnson (she was the woman who broke the news) had entered the room. Until then it had seemed full of sunlight and laughter and afterwards it was a dark and gloomy place. Cave like. She thought of Matty, deep below the ground; she still had hours to wait for him to come home. She stopped what she was doing and sat in, what had become, her chair by the fire, and for the first time since her wedding day, she wept; on what should be a joyous day, she cried. There was a hint of panic to her tears and it took her some time to regain control, which she eventually did by thinking about the others who'd been in the room that morning. They had lived with the knowledge of the dangers their husbands faced all their lives. It was only now, because she was an outsider that she began to realise what being the wife of a miner meant. The daily uncertainty, would he or wouldn't he come home. Knowing his life depended on a timber prop that your father, or someone just like him, who spent his life out in the open air, and not in some coal dust filled cavern, had dragged out of a wood. She cast these thoughts from her mind; she couldn't allow herself to think like that. She'd done enough of that over Walter. She had news for Matty. Good news. She mustn't let him see her upset. He'd kept the dangers of his job from her for a reason, he didn't want her worrying about him. So she must not let him see her worried. She must get over this. She must be like the others or she would drive herself mad. It was at this time that Betty thought back to Matty's words on grief when they'd discussed Walter's mother and her attitude to the gypsy woman's prophecy. She began, then, to understand what Matty had meant. He had obviously seen grief more than once during his life as a miner, today was proof of that. He would feel for the men who'd been lost today, even though he probably never knew them. They were like him, they were miners, doing the same jobs, in the same conditions and facing the same dangers. Yes, Matty had felt grief, many times. He understood Walter's mother better than she.

That night after his bath, she gave Matty the news and he was overjoyed. She'd cooked a meat and potato pie, his favourite, to celebrate, and they sat late into the night talking about whether it would be a boy or a girl and about respective names. It was only later as they got ready for bed that the accident was mentioned by him. Three men had died, he said, in a roof collapse. He mentioned it almost as an aside. It was never mentioned again.

In July Betty gave birth to an eight pound six ounce baby boy, and, as predicted, Annie Clegg helped with the birth, while Matty paced up and down the back yard, until called in by Annie to hold the newcomer. The child was christened, Walter Mathew; the name was Matty's idea, and Betty's friends, old and new came to the little terraced house, spilling over into the yard behind, for the occasion. Life was good for the Campbell family in 1922. A year later almost to the day the group assembled again for a similar celebration. Edward Kenneth Campbell was christened: 1923 another good year for Betty and family.

CHAPTER FIFTEEN.

1923. That year a man was admitted to a convalescent home in Hampshire. He'd been lucky considering some of the places wounded ex-soldiers were taken to after WW1. The doctor in charge of the home, Dr. Freddy Pearce, was a forward thinking man, who was trying to understand the effects of shell shock on the men who had fought in the Great War. Many had been shot for cowardice, but Dr Pearce thought they'd been suffering from shell shock and executing them was wrong, and intended to prove it.

The man had been found working on a farm in Belgium. The old farmer's wife suffering from dementia had begun threatening travellers with a shotgun on the road, and the police had been called. Living in an outbuilding they discovered what at first they took to be a tramp. On closer inspection they found he was a foreigner who had been working on the farm. They took him, along with the old lady to the local hospital. In her more lucid moments the old lady explained that her husband had found the man wandering about the fields, in just his vest, trousers and wearing one boot. She told her listeners to verify her story with her husband who, they all knew, had been dead many years. They'd taken him in she said, but he couldn't speak French or Flemish and he was wandering in the mind. This caused a kindly smile among her listeners. They fed him and clothed him and he began to work on the farm. He obviously had knowledge of the work, and as they were both getting on in years the stranger was a great help to them. Both of their sons had been lost in the war and they were now struggling to keep up with the work. The stranger was strong and seemed to know what he was doing. He was a godsend. He helped them a lot. When she was asked why they never reported finding the man to the authorities, The old lady said nothing other than she had dressed his wounds, had fed him and clothed him in their son's old clothes. Try as they might they could get nothing more out of her. Except an entreaty to ask her husband.

The stranger was filthy. His hair was long, knotted and streaked with grey. He was unshaven, his beard reaching to his waist was also knotted and stained with food. His toe nails curled under his feet causing him pain as he walked in his oversized boots. The nails had caused ulcers under his feet where they'd dug in. He was covered in lice and had weeping sores over most of his body. He was badly undernourished and dehydrated. His mind was wandering as the old lady had said. The doctor who checked the man out spoke a little English, having worked with the allies in field hospitals during the Great War. He became convinced that his patient was an Englishman and he reported his suspicions to his superiors. The man was months recovering and in all that time he rarely spoke. During this period the farmer's wife died, and with her all links to his past died also. It was 1920.

When the authorities became involved a local bureaucrat was sent to question him. Upon discovering that the man was almost totally deaf the case was handed over to a different department, his area of expertise having nothing to do with the disabled.

The bureaucrat registered the stranger as a Belgian deaf person when he handed the case over. His thinking was that the man had been made homeless during the hostilities, and had stumbled across the farm during his wanderings, and made his home in the out-buildings where he'd been discovered. Almost everything the old lady had said was dismissed as senile ravings.

The doctor who had originally treated him and reported his case to the authorities was not convinced and persisted in seeing the patient much to the chagrin of the people whose job it was to try to rehabilitate him. The doctor insisted on keeping in touch with the stranger, saying that the man was his patient. As the ulcers on his feet were slow in healing he was allowed access.

Slowly, over time, the doctor began to reach the stranger. By speaking to him in English, for part of the visit, at every meeting, he finally got a reply. The doctor had told the man his name was Georges. His reward was, one day to be called, in a very croaky, and much unused voice, 'Dr. George'. And to have his hand shaken in a vice like grip, by a very calloused and dirt ingrained hand. Dr. George swallowed hard to rid himself of the lump which rose in his throat, finally all his perseverance had borne fruit. He had reached his patient. Now the real work could begin. It was January 1921.

Once the man started to talk, the Doctor visited him every day. The stranger would only talk to 'Dr. George', as he insisted on calling him. He didn't mind anyone listening, but if the listener asked a question, or spoke, the man would shut up and that would be the end of the session for that day. No amount of persuasion would change the outcome. The only person he allowed to speak to him, or ask him questions, was Dr. George. Over the year Dr. George managed to get the man to tell him everything he could remember, which at first was very little: mainly about his grueling life on the old lady's farm. Dr. George listened, wanting to ask about how the man reached the farm, but knowing he had to let the healing process he'd set in motion run its excruciatingly, slow course.

At first, the stranger began, life on the farm had been good. He had been cared for, and he was just beginning to be able to do small jobs around the place, when the old couple's health began to deteriorate, and his life had again become a fight for survival.

It was the old woman who first became strange. Some days she would feed him, calling him Frank; he thought that was the name she used, but he wasn't sure, because of her strong accent. Other days she would run him off. The old man at these times would placate her, and things would return to normal, or what he thought of as normal at that time. He had been given a room in the farmhouse, which, the old man said, had been the couple's son's room. He was told to use what clothes he wanted from the wardrobe. The shoes, and boots were too big, but they were all that he had, so he wore them. It was not long after he began to dress in these clothes that the old lady began to call him Frank.

The old man would take him out in the morning and show him the jobs he wanted him to do. He noticed that the old lady's condition worsened. She became more and more confused as time went by, sometimes becoming violent towards the old man. If he tried to intervene she would turn on him, also, so he began to keep out of her way, communicating only through the old man. It was after one of these confrontations between the couple, when he returned in the evening from mending an outbuildings roof, that he was met in the fold-yard by the old man sporting a black eye and bruised face. The old man told him he couldn't come inside the house for the time being, and that he'd left his food for him in the barn. The old man was upset, and said he was sorry, but the old lady was confused and he expected she would be all right again soon. He turned away and went indoors. The stranger said that the old man's health deteriorated rapidly after that. He found his food where the old man had left it along with a blanket. That's when he started to live in the barn.

The old man continued to find him work, which he continued to do, all the time getting stronger and slowly regaining his health. But as he was getting better, the old man was getting weaker. He found that his food, which the old man was still leaving for him, was now usually only a sandwich, which he suspected had been prepared by the old man. Sometimes he thought it might even be the old man's own food. He began to look for ways of escaping from the place, walking miles over the fields, but this only proved to him that he was still weak and disoriented. He didn't know where he was, and he never saw anyone else except the old couple, generally, the old man. He hadn't seen the old lady for over a week now. He was working on the garden plot when he heard the gunshot. It upset him greatly, it frightened him, he remembered, and he ran to the barn and cowered there for the rest of that day, and all the next. He saw no one, and the old man never brought him any food after that. It was maybe two days, or two weeks, he couldn't remember, until he had enough nerve to venture out of the barn again, in daylight. At first it was only at night he crept out in search of food but he always returned before daybreak.

He'd been eating whatever food he could scavenge from around the house and fields, turnips, raw mostly, which he pulled as he wanted them, hiding when he heard any noise at all. He continued to live in the barn, still hoping that the old man would begin to bring him food again. He knew his health was getting worse. He'd developed a cough, and his skin was breaking out in sores, which he thought were rat bites, but he had nowhere else to go. It was getting really cold at night now. Frost covered the fields most nights.

When he saw her next, she staggered from the door, with the shotgun under her arm. He'd been hiding in the barn, watching the house, to see if he could see the old man. The old lady was in a disheveled state. Her grey hair, was tangled and hung down her back. Her clothes were dirty and she was unwashed. He'd never seen her like that before. She was shouting for 'Frank'. He slowly emerged from the barn and when she saw him it was as if nothing had happened. "Frank", she called and waved him to her. "Something's happened to your father." She went back into the house. At first he didn't know what to do but hunger drove him to follow her. When he entered the place he immediately knew what the gunshot had been. The old lady stood by the filthy sink, looking down at the corpse of her husband, whom she had shot in the chest. He lay by the burned out fire, across the hearth, one arm had been badly burned when it had fallen into the flames on the day he was shot. The fire had never been used again. The stranger hoped he'd been dead when the arm entered the flames. It appeared that the old lady had been living on whatever she could find in the cupboards. Empty boxes and cartons littered the room. There was a chewed chicken carcass, and some empty cans, one with blood around the rim where the old lady had cut herself when opening it. He couldn't see how she'd opened the cans, but she had. The room, which was freezing cold, was filled with rubbish collected from all over the house, or so it appeared to him: there were clothes and pictures, old photographs, pots and pans, all unwashed, and everywhere there was filth. She'd been using the corner of the room as a toilet and the place stank, even in the cold there were flies.

"What's wrong with him?" she asked.

As he turned to answer she raised the gun and screamed at him to get out. He ducked and ran for the door, luckily, the gun was empty. She'd never thought to reload it. But now he just ran back to the barn, terrified, wondering what he could do. And more to the point, what she would do. That night she stood in the doorway and fired the gun into the barn, scattering splinters from the door. She'd found the cartridges and she knew how to load it. That's how things progressed from then on. Some days she would be fine, and he would be able to get food, others she would try to kill him and he would have to hide where he could. All the time she was deteriorating mentally; so was he. Finally he was as far back as when the couple had first found him. He'd become no more than an animal, barely surviving among the outbuildings. This was as far as the doctor could get with the man, and it took him many weeks to get this far.

The above is roughly a transcript of a report Dr. George gave to the psychiatrists working on the unknown man's case. He had taken into account the difficulty all concerned had with language and translation. The man had very little French and the old couple had a little Flemish but spoke French as their main language, so some liberties were taken by the doctor in his interpretation of what he was hearing. He took into account what he learned from the police who answered the call and what he'd been told by others who'd worked on the case. All in all he felt that he'd managed to work out what happened to the man at the farm accurately. The psychiatrist, who sat in on some of the interviews agreed and between them they worked out a strategy to take the stranger on to the second phase of his recovery. They envisioned taking the man back mentally, to the place he was before he reached the farm; it was here that the difficulties arose.

As Dr. George slowly tried to get the man to remember how he got onto the old people's farm he stubbornly refused to talk about that time in his life. He would talk about England and his life there. This was a pyrrhic victory for the doctor, in that it proved his earlier belief that the man was English, other than that it proved nothing. It was obvious to all concerned, and everyone agreed without dissent, that the man was an English soldier suffering from shell shock; the problem was proving it. They needed some kind of proof to get the man repatriated. Without it the English would not accept that they had a soldier missing that they hadn't accounted for. Every soldier in the theatre of battle where this man could have fought, had been properly accounted for. As far as the English were concerned they had no one missing. The problem was the Belgians'. Lots of people spoke English, that didn't make them English, was the British War Office view.

It was decided after much soul searching, to just let the man talk. The group working on his recovery were convinced that they needed to keep his mind working chronologically backwards, in order that, when he was, hopefully, fully cured he would have a proper perspective on what had happened to him. Their belief was that if he were allowed just to jump from one memory to the next, as he wanted to, he would bury all his worst memories, and that they would come back, in the years to come to haunt him, causing him to break down again. They wanted him, for his own good, to leave them, having re-lived everything that had put him there, and with nothing buried in his mind that could haunt him in the future. They believed that if he could do that, face his demons now, he would be fully cured. Their problem was how to get him to do it!

So it was reluctantly that Dr. George allowed his patient to talk freely about any subject he chose. The man chose to talk about doves, or to be precise, one dove in particular. After the first, free talking session, the group were even more convinced that their man was a soldier. They believed his dove, was the dove of peace, and that his references to it was a cry for help, from the battlefield. They were now convinced that they were on the right track, all their earlier reluctance vanished and they wanted him to talk about the dove, as they were sure now it would lead them to his wartime exploits, and how he ended up at the farm.

The next session started with high expectations from the whole team. It began with the soldier talking about his place of work in England and about his building a dovecote. He then talked about meeting his dove and taking her to the dovecote and explaining to her how he'd built it. He described sitting and watching all the other birds flying in and out of this cote with his dove. It took the good doctor some time to work out that the dove he was talking about was a person. Dove was a pet name for his girlfriend. When this dawned on him he realized that the soldier had gone back to the best time of his life. He wasn't on the battlefield, he was where he'd felt safest, and happiest before the war.

This session caused a great amount of despondency to settle on the group. But they, after much discussion, decided that now they had set out on this course they must follow it through, to try to backtrack now would probably do more damage than good. They had no choice but to continue.

And so the sessions continued. The soldier as he was now know to them, talked lovingly about 'Dove'; they never heard him refer to her as anything else, but it was obviously the love of his life. Slowly he revealed how he'd hurt his 'Dove' by enlisting in the army. Here they had the first reference to his being a soldier. This revelation caused a great deal of celebration among the psychiatric group working with Dr. George.

Slowly now, he began to tell them of his life after he joined up. Referring back regularly to his pain at hurting 'Dove', he covered his training and his journey to the continent. His first encounters with the enemy, and the first of his friends to die. He covered a lot of very painful ground, but he never told them to which company he belonged, or his own name. They allowed him to talk on, hoping that one day this information would come out. Some days he was very voluble, others he was more taciturn, reliving the experiences in his own head before just giving the barest details of what had happened. These times were the most painful, for all concerned, especially the soldier, who during these sessions regularly broke down, and had to be taken back to his room.

Over the year Dr. George finally had some kind of picture of what had happened to the man, albeit in places a little sketchy. He had described a group of young men, all friends, and from the same area joining up together to great fanfare. They'd been led to war by a charismatic leader who had promised them great things, and home for Christmas. He had described all of these friends dying, leaving five only alive. These five had been forced to join a rag-tag group of similar 'Pals', he'd called them, remnants of other such groups as his own. These men had been moved from one area of the front to another as they'd been needed. They'd moved around so much that they didn't know where they were in the end. They'd watched many more of their new friends die in the mud and gore of the battlefield, but the remaining five had somehow managed to survive and stay together. He then talked of this ragbag group being moved again and spread out along the trenches; they'd been told that the end of the war was close and the five friends had managed to stay together eating rabbit. This reference to rabbit had baffled the Doctors for some time until one of them decided it must have been some code that they'd been told to use, suggesting they were some kind of intelligence unit. One of the team had spent some time in London and said the term 'Rabbit' was a colloquial term for talk; it was probably meaningless now. The rest of the group agreed, bowing to their colleague's superior knowledge. They also agreed that they had enough information now to contact the War Office again. The references they had gathered from the soldier about his whereabouts during the fighting and his mention of the 'Pals' was enough for them to work out a timeline and prove that he was a British soldier. Once this information was received in Britain, and checked against their records, the War Office, much against their better judgment, reluctantly sent a psychiatrist from a convalescent home in England to interview the soldier.

Once this interview had been conducted towards the end of 1921, preparations were immediately started to repatriate the young man. The interviewing psychiatrist from England had obviously been moved by what he'd heard and thanked the Belgian team for all the work they'd done, and for all the help they'd given to the injured, and now acknowledged, British, soldier. His emphasis on British was for their benefit, and they appreciated his acknowledgement greatly.

Before the young man left for his home country, Dr. George ensured that he would be allowed to see his charge once he'd got back home. The visiting doctor assured him that he would always be welcome to visit whenever he wanted to. And so it was with conflicting feelings that the young man and Dr. George, as he would always be known to him, left each other. After hugging one another on the steps of the hospital where he'd lived for so long, he began his long journey home.

He would always limp: not only because of the ulcers under his feet which were now healed, but because he'd had a small piece of shrapnel embedded in his leg for the duration of his time on the farm. This had been removed by the hospital but it had caused permanent damage to the right leg.

He had no idea how it had got there. His right ear drum was burst and he had impaired hearing in his left. Nothing at all could be done for that except for him to wear a hearing aid. He was alive that was the main thing. Now, the psychiatrist who travelled back with him said, all they had to do was to get his memory back. They needed to find out who he was, who 'Dove' was and where he came from; he was sure there were people in England who would be ecstatic at his return.

When Walter landed in Dover it was 1923, eight years after leaving to fight in a war he'd been promised would be over by Christmas. The Walter that returned didn't even know who he was. He boarded a taxi with the psychiatrist who had been his constant, travelling companion since he left Belgium. They travelled to the convalescent home in Hampshire, much of the way in silence, as Walter tried to take in what he was seeing after such a long time away. As he walked down the pathway to the front door of the white painted building, he noticed how beautifully scented the roses were that bordered the path. They were in full bloom.

CHAPTER SIXTEEN.

Walter soon got into the routine at the convalescent home. The men slept four or six to a room normally, depending on how far along the road to recovery they were. There was also a hospital wing where the severely injured were treated. It was now so long after the war that there were few hospital beds taken and the recovering invalids each had a room of their own. Walter, who was called George by the staff, after the doctor who'd given him so much help in Belgium, had sessions of physiotherapy, each morning to help with his walking, and to try to build muscle and strengthen his lame leg. Afternoons, at first, were given over to intensive psychiatric sessions with the doctor who'd travelled home with him. The intention being to carry on where the work had left off in Belgium. But it soon became evident that this approach wasn't working. 'George', as he was now known didn't seem to want to remember. He seemed perfectly happy with life where he was. The psychiatrist was afraid of a relapse, but there was nothing he could do without his patient's help. In the evenings it was noted that the patient known as 'George' would help the old man who tended the gardens and so in order to keep the invalid occupied the afternoon sessions were scrapped and 'George' was allowed to help in the garden instead. The psychiatrist had to admit that the gardening was more therapeutic than the one to one talking sessions had been. The doctor was still worried about any deeply held memories and so once a fortnight the two men sat down, informally and just chatted, or that's what the doctor had told 'George'. The doctor subtly managed to get 'George' talking about his early life and slowly managed to drag out of him some of his buried memories. This approach took a great deal of time but it was certainly working. The more 'George' became engrossed in his gardening work, the more he opened up at the informal sessions.

The old gardener was appreciative of the help also and the two men got along famously. A breakthrough came when 'George' asked the old man if he could plant out a vegetable plot. Up until then the gardens had been purely decorative. Permission was given and a plot was allocated along the side of the building, facing south. It wasn't a big plot, but to be honest, it was all that the injured man could handle at that moment in time. 'George' spent most of his time, when not helping the old gardener now, on this plot. He planted spring cabbage, carrots, beetroot and onions, it was obvious from the way the garden prospered that he knew what he was doing and it was during an informal talk when the vegetable plot was mentioned that 'George' became Walter again.

The psychiatrist asked him about his gardening skills, and completely out of the blue he mentioned his father being head gardener at the Manor. Where the Manor was located was still a mystery, but the psychiatrist, recognizing the importance of what had just been revealed allowed 'George' to continue. He told about his work with his father and during the conversation mentioned his father calling him by name, "'Walter', he would shout if he couldn't see me. I used to hide in the greenhouses just to get his goat, at times." Walter grinned, enjoying the memories.

"Did your father ever find out, Walter?" asked the man in order to use his given name.

"No. I don't think he ever did."

Walter stopped. His face clouded over as memories came flooding back. He stood up, causing the heavy fabric, covered easy chair, he'd been reclining in, to fall over backwards with the force. He moaned and thrust his face into his hands. His shoulders began to shake and tears fell from between his fingers onto the parquet flooring. A breakthrough had been made.

It took Walter, as everyone now had to call him at every opportunity, a few days to recover from that incident. He wanted to talk to the psychiatrist again as soon as the shock was over but the man knew that if he allowed Walter to gabble on with the thoughts now flooding his head, much could be lost. He advised Walter to rest, quietly in his room for the evening; it was now after five o'clock, and he said they'd talk again the following day. He hoped that by doing this Walter would be able to assimilate the memories filling his mind and that in doing so, more memories would come to the fore.

This didn't prove to be the case, at first, and the doctor was disappointed. What did happen was that Walter's mind filled in all the little details around his father and mother, his brothers, and his job as handyman at the Manor came to light. He remembered building a dovecote. But that was it. He couldn't remember his brothers' names or where the Manor was, but he could remember taking apart an old broken down wagon and using the wood to build a dovecote, and then he used an old trap to build a bench. Walter was overjoyed at this recovered memory and the psychiatrist realized that this was a great moment in Walter's life and, also, a giant step in his recovery.

Walter's next request was to build a dovecote. The doctor authorized this as part of Walter's therapy, and soon Walter was hard at work with a load of timber on the unplanted area of his plot building the cote. The hospital didn't have a workshop that Walter could use, but this didn't deter him in the least. Quickly, it seemed to the doctor the dovecote began to take shape. During this time it was deemed by the powers that be, who ran the convalescent home for the War Office that Walter was now fully functional and could be released into society.

The psychiatrist argued that he still had a lot of work to do with Walter in order for him to fully recover his mind and not to relapse. The War Office countered that the man was taking up a bed that could be used by someone else and also valuable monetary resources. The psychiatrist replied, totally exasperated by the bureaucrats, at this juncture, that the hospital was half empty and the convalescent home had only six men in it, and beds for twenty. The bureaucrat's reply was that numbers were not the point. The psychiatrist, now completely at the end of his tether with this red tape offered Walter the job of assistant gardener at the home, which he gladly accepted. The doctor then informed the War Office that Walter was rehabilitated and had a job as a gardener. This satisfied the bureaucrats, allowed Walter to be paid for his work, and allowed the psychiatrist to continue his work with Walter. Everyone was happy. Walter stayed in his room and was fed with the patients as normal. But now he earned a wage; all that the office in the home had to do, was change the name of the room Walter occupied, to assistant gardener's room, and remove room ten from the hospital log. His wages came out of the maintenance budget, which the War Office covered anyway. No one was the wiser, and no one ever questioned the alterations.

While this little contretemps was going on Walter completed the dovecote. What it needed now was painting. Every room in the hospital was painted white, so acquiring the paint was not a problem; it meant the dovecote was painted white, which was a vast improvement on the green he'd used originally. It was during the painting period that Walter began to think about raising the dovecote and positioning it on the grounds. This brought about his next flood of memories. This remembrance was not as dramatic as the first, but it was just as meaningful. Walter searched out his psychiatrist to tell him what he had remembered, which in itself the doctor said was a step in the right direction. Now that Walter was an employee of the home as opposed to being a patient, officially anyway, the doctor insisted he call him Freddy. He did this for two reasons: if anyone from the War Office did come to check up on the new gardener's assistant, he wanted the meeting between them to be as informal as possible. Secondly, he wanted Walter to feel comfortable around him, he wanted to have as near as possible, the same relationship with Walter as Dr. George had; he felt that this was the way to take Walter now. To be just two friends talking. He hoped that way Walter would open up more. And more rapidly. The approach seemed to work, although it took Walter a while to get used to his doctor being called Freddy.

Walter explained to Freddy that while he was painting the dovecote he was thinking about fixing the pole to the underside to lift the thing up. It was at that moment that he thought they didn't have a blacksmith. The blacksmith thought was the catalyst. He remembered then that the dovecote from his past, had a bracket made for it by the blacksmith that worked on the Manor. He described in detail what he'd designed for the blacksmith to make, he even drew it out on the doctor's pad. He then described squaring the round pole off to fit into the bracket. The blacksmith's name, he said was Mr. Asquith. His own brother's names were Albert, who was the oldest and David the youngest; his surname was Blower. After this revelation Walter sat back and sighed a sigh of utter relief, as if a great load had been lifted from his shoulders.

Freddy knew that after this knowledge entered Walter's mind and settled there would be repercussions. He could see from Walter's demeanor that the enormity of what had happened hadn't yet hit him. He still didn't remember where the Manor was, but Freddy thought he may now have enough information about Walter to use War Office files to find it out himself. He advised Walter to rest now as he had done before in order to allow his mind to assimilate the new information, which Walter gladly did.

After that day, which to Freddy's surprise didn't cause Walter any problems, Walter began to remember something almost daily. Little things mostly but occasionally things of moment. But each memory was a vital part of the jigsaw that was Walter's life.

Using the drawing from Freddy's pad a bracket was made by a blacksmith in the town nearby and a piece of four inch by four inch square timber was acquired to fit in the blacksmith's bracket. After all these preparations, two months after Walter began building the dovecote, some burly chaps, acquaintances of the blacksmith, lifted it into position at the front of the hall. A number of the staff were standing by to applaud and this again brought to Walter's mind the inauguration ceremony organized by the Major and his wife for the original dovecote. This memory did cause Walter problems, because within this memory he saw Betty. Walter fainted.

The blacksmith's men completed the siting of the dovecote while Freddy and his staff looked after Walter. Walter was carried back into the hospital and placed on a ward, while they brought him round. During this process he rambled on about the Major, the lads and mainly about Betty. When he was fully recovered, he seemed put out to be in the hospital. Freddy explained what had happened and asked him about the people he'd mentioned. Walter was at a complete loss, he could remember nothing of what had passed. Freddy didn't press him because he believed that what had just happened was a big moment in Walter's recovery. He fully expected, now, sooner rather than later for Walter to fully recover his memory. The key was the dovecote: whatever Walter wanted to do with or around the dovecote Freddy would allow. A few days later Walter requested timber for a bench and a half dozen doves. Freddy complied.

That evening he wrote a letter to Dr. George informing him of what had happened that day. Up until that moment he had tried not to raise the doctor's hopes too much, knowing how much effort he'd put into Walter's recovery. But this letter was different; he felt for the first time that soon something positive would happen, and he had to tell someone of his excitement. Dr. George was the obvious choice as they both had so much invested in Walter's recovery. Both of them felt Water to be a remarkable young man, not only because of what he'd survived (to survive at all was a remarkable achievement) but to have done it with such humility and humour. He'd carried his wounds, both mental and physical with such good grace, nothing had seemed to be too much for him; both doctors wanted nothing more for Walter than a full recovery. It was no more than such a brave person as he, deserved. He hoped Dr. George would reply quickly; he would value his input, he thought, as he sealed the envelope and switched off his desk light.

The following day the timber arrived for the bench and Walter began work immediately. Two days later the doves arrived and Walter began training them to use the cote. It was an exact replica of the first one he'd built and as he fixed the wire around it trapping the doves in for the next couple of weeks, memories came flooding back to him. He shook them off, wanting to finish his bench, but the memories would not go away. That night his sleep was plagued by dreams.

Disjointed memories, doves filled the air and amongst them, seemingly flying with them, bright white, flaming stars. Men in uniform clapping and drinking wine, celebrating something, while others drank beer from glass mugs. Always the doves filled the air, cooing and swirling round, feathers everywhere. Then rabbits, there were rabbits and bright shining stars. There was mud and blood, noise. Men and horses screaming in agony. Gunshots and shell-fire. Screams, always there were the screams. He woke up kicking and sweating profusely. His sheets were in a pile on the floor. He hoped he hadn't been shouting and woken anyone up. It had been a long time since he'd had a dream like that. He didn't want another nightmare any time soon. Tomorrow he would complete the bench, then maybe his dreams would go away and leave him with only memories.

CHAPTER SEVENTEEN.

Walter had completed his bench and removed the wire from the dovecote. He sat down now on it, where it had been placed against the wall of the garden to catch the evening sun. It was warm and Walter decided for a moment, to watch the birds. They had grown accustomed to the cote and were swooping in and out. He was pleased; soon, he hoped they would lay eggs and have young, then he would feel his dovecote was a success. The sun made him sleepy and his eyes closed. Behind him a gentle breeze rippled through the ivy leaves which climbed along the top of the wall and the roses scented the air. Walter felt at peace as he drifted off to sleep.

***

He was in the back of a lorry, his friends were with him, they were laughing and waving, people were waving back. They were drinking beer, celebrating the boys' departure, as if it was something good. He could see his father, and Betty was with him; they didn't seem to be joining in the celebrations. Next came the Major; he was crying. He couldn't move and his horse had disappeared. He was screaming covered from head to foot in gore. He only had one hand. Cyril, his friend was screaming, he'd been shot in the face; the noise filled his head. Cyril had been with him when he met Betty, at the fair. They were throwing grenades at coconuts. He was with some of his friends, they were laughing at the helter-skelter slide.

The slide became a water filled shell hole, the men sliding down its sides into the grey mud; it exploded; they were blown up in the trench. Everywhere was mud and filth. Men he didn't know and men he did, were all crying covered in mud and pieces of other people; skin, and brains, and bone, and limbs. Everywhere were bits of men he'd known, all with faces and all the eyes looking at him.

Men were scratching at the lice crawling all over them, in their hair and clothing, everywhere there was a mixture of blood, gore and mud. There was a loud explosion, and then the gas. Some men didn't manage to get their masks on, their eyes were popping out like frogs. Silence. There was silence now. It was dark, a black starless sky, and then there was a star. One bright shining star in the black sky. Walter was afraid of the star. He didn't know why, but he was terrified. He was with four friends, they were in a farm without a roof. They could see the sky where the roof should be. They had built a fire in the middle of this roofless building using timbers from the damaged roof. One of the men held up a dead rabbit by its back legs. Walter took the rabbit from his friend. He took off his battledress and shirt. He was wearing a dirty vest, they were all laughing. He saw the star in the sky and was afraid again. He screamed and dropped to the floor. He was laughing again with his friends, he didn't know why he was frightened. He went outside to clean the rabbit. His friends were boiling water over the fire in the middle of the floor. Walter walked to the horse trough outside in the farm yard and with a knife he started to open the rabbit up, to clean it for the pot, as he had seen his father do many times before. Then he saw the star in the sky. He knew now what it was, it was a ranging flare from the German artillery. The farm exploded with his friends inside. The shock wave threw him up in the air, one of his boots came off, the left one he remembered. He was turning and rolling in the air. All around him, hitting him, there were bricks and stones and the ever present mud, he hit the ground, rolling over and over in the detritus from the explosion. He couldn't remember how or where he landed. He woke up screaming again laid across the bench. Freddy was there holding his hands to stop him hurting himself as he'd thrashed about in his fear. "It's OK, Walter. It's OK."

Walter slept for two full days once they got him back to his room. When he awoke he had his full memory back. He could remember everything that had happened to him. There were no gaps. Walter wished sometimes there were.

At the next session Walter told Freddy everything. He told of the Belgians at the farm. They had lost two sons in France in the conflict. He believed that loss was what had tipped the old lady over the edge. The final group in the roofless farmhouse had been led to understand that the war was over by an excited officer, who'd gone along the line spreading the news. They had managed to get a rabbit from somewhere and had drawn lots as to who would clean it. Walter lost. They weren't bothered about the smoke from the blazing fire believing, because of what the officer had told them, that the war was over. When Walter took off his battledress, to go and clean the rabbit, he'd inadvertently left all his identification in the pockets. So when the blasted building was checked for casualties, they found what was left of Walter's comrades and what was left of his battledress among the mangled corpses. They looked no further, human remains and bits of five uniforms. That was all they needed. Walter was missing presumed killed along with the others.

He'd seen the Major get injured. As the man had promised he stayed with his men, even at the front. He'd seen his comrades gassed. That was a memory too far for Walter. He refused to go on after that, but Freddy knew at that point, that Walter had all of his memories back, and left his interrogation at that. There would be no more sessions unless Walter requested them. Which he never did.

Walter recuperated rapidly after that. It had taken ten years for him to recover, and he pottered around the garden for a while considering his next move. He desperately wanted to see Betty again, and his parents, but Freddy advised caution. Ten years was a long time, he warned. People would have gotten used to his being dead. They would have moved on with their lives. He told Walter that, although in his mind now, it was like yesterday, to his loved ones, it would be a great shock for them to see him alive and well after a decade. Freddy suggested writing first to pave the way as he put it. But Walter thought that might be as great a shock as seeing him. He said he would ponder on the question for a while and they left the decision for a later date. Walter went back to his gardening and Freddy worried about what Walter would do, as it was obvious he wanted to surprise his loved ones. Freddy knew this was the wrong thing to do and contemplated writing the letter himself but he couldn't do that to Walter. He'd have to leave the final decision to him.

After a number of discussions with Freddy, Walter came up with a plan he thought was best all round. He decided he would travel back to the village and have a look around, just to see what had happened in his absence. He wouldn't approach anyone, and he wouldn't make his presence known. He would just reconnoiter; he smiled at using the military term. He didn't believe anyone would recognize him anyway, he thought he'd changed so much. That was what he wanted to do, Freddy tried to dissuade him, but he was adamant. Once he'd seen how the land lay he would then make up his mind about writing, or just going to see people. The person he was thinking about was Betty, as Freddy well knew. Walter had talked about virtually no one else once he'd remembered her name.

So it was that on a warm, but overcast day Walter set off on the long journey from Hampshire to his home on the Yorkshire/Nottinghamshire border. He carried all his worldly belongings in a battered, old brown, pressed cardboard suitcase tied with string because he didn't trust the catches. Freddy had arranged travel passes for him, for both coach and train. The journey would take him two days; with a stopover at Leicester to make a connection. When Freddy saw the battered brown case he knew Walter's intentions, and he felt Walter was making a mistake, but there was nothing he could do.

The journey was uneventful. He enjoyed travelling on the steam train, but then he'd always liked trains. From the railway station he caught a bus to the town he now remembered and knew so well. The bus trip was a journey back in time for Walter. Very little seemed to have changed and he found himself hoping this was going to be the case all down the line. At the bus terminus he disembarked, wearing the pin striped suit Freddy had acquired for him and a trilby hat. His tie, shirt and shoes he'd bought himself. Over his arm he carried a gabardine Macintosh although he questioned the need for it, hot as it was, at the height of the British summer.

Walter was thirsty and a little peckish. The sandwiches he'd purchased at his overnight stop had long gone, his flask of tea long drunk. So he decided to call at the terminus buffet for a cup of tea before catching the bus onward, the five miles to the village. He checked first that the bus stop to the village was still outside the terminus, which it was. It stood as it always had, two hundred yards to the left opposite the main post office. The street hadn't changed a bit. Walter felt the familiar pull of homesickness as he looked around his old home town. Everything looked in need of a coat of paint but otherwise it was unchanged. He walked back into the bus station and entered the buffet. He placed his coat and hat on a bench, set near the white marble-topped counter, and ordered a tea.

"Cup or mug?" asked the pretty girl behind the counter, her auburn hair held out of her eyes with a tartan head scarf tied in a turban.

"Mug please." He smiled.

Walter sat down with his purchase and savoured the strong taste of the tea, from the large, heavy white mug. Walter looked around the room, basking in the normality of what he was doing after the trauma of what he'd been through. He found it hard to stop smiling. The room was painted light green and had a high white ceiling. The wall opposite where he sat was un-plastered brick also painted in the light green colour. High up near the ceiling was a row of windows which allowed natural light into the room. Suspended from the ceiling and following the aisle between the tables hung a row of three white globes. These were the electric lights which lit the place. These, Walter noticed were switched on. To his right was the door through which he'd entered. This wall was half wood, and the top half was glass as was the wall against which he leant drinking his now almost empty mug of tea. To his left was another door which led into the buffet directly from the terminus. This door opened alongside the counter where the girl in the tartan headscarf reigned supreme over her steaming coffee and tea machines. Walter enjoyed taking all of this in. He was enjoying his mug of tea, and just the plain ordinariness of what he was doing immensely. Walter looked along the counter to the right of the girl where stood some glass fronted shelves which held her stock of sandwiches and sweet cakes. There were only three other people in the room. A couple, who like Walter were enjoying mugs of tea, and a bus conductor who sat alone and appeared to be on his break.

The girl behind the counter had now been joined by another girl who had on the uniform of a waitress. Walter thought it a little extravagant to employ a waitress in such a small place. After a few words with the counter girl the waitress began clearing the tables and wiping them down with a clean white cloth. Walter finished his tea and contemplated another, he had enjoyed the first one so much, and maybe a sandwich to go with it. As he stood mug in hand, a movement to his right caught his eye near the door through which he'd entered the room. He looked through the glass unbelieving. It was Betty, just as he remembered her, unchanged. She was walking out of the bus station. He almost dropped his mug. It clattered down so noisily onto the table that everyone looked towards him. He grabbed his case and coat and rushed to the door, just as he reached it and pulled it open towards him he heard someone calling him. "Sir. Sir." He looked back over his shoulder desperate to get out, the little waitress was running up the aisle holding his hat out to him, "You left your hat, sir." She handed it to him.

"Thanks." He took it from her, flustered. Everyone in the place was looking at him. He rushed out of the buffet and headed towards the large, arched stone entrance to the bus station. The swift, unaccustomed movement, causing him some pain in his damaged leg. He looked quickly to the left, towards the bus stop to the village where he expected to see her.

There was a crowd at the stop, he thought he recognised some of the faces, but they were all looking expectantly down the road; no one even glanced towards him. He couldn't see Betty amongst them. There were two other great stone arches, before the pavement arced round and then ran along a low, metal railed wall alongside the northern road out of the town. He looked, but there was no one at all that way. He looked across the road to the row of shops and the post office. The shops were busy, crowded with people. It was impossible to spot an individual among the throng. His leg was aching now, badly, but he ignored it and kept looking, hoping against hope that he would spot her. Now, from the junction came the single decker bus which would take the crowd at the bus stop to the village. Automatically he turned back towards the stop, and there she was! She was just standing up from a crouching position. She brushed her hand through a toddler's hair as she stood. She must have been tying his shoelace or something like that, when he'd first looked and he'd missed her. The bus noisily pulled up at the stop, screeching brakes, in a blue, petrol fumed haze, as he called her name. She didn't hear his call because of the noise. She picked up the child and handed him to a man standing near her. She then took charge of a pushchair, folding it up and expertly taking its passenger in her arms, resting the infant on her hip, as the man with her now took the folded pushchair in his free hand. The family, for it was obvious to Walter now, that they were a family, boarded the bus, followed by the rest of the queue. Walter set off as fast as his painful leg would carry him towards the waiting bus, but then he stopped and put down his case. The driver waited a second. Walter could see his face in the circular wing mirror. Walter waved him to leave, which he did, in the same noisy fume-filled way. Walter stood and watched the bus as it travelled down the main street to the bend, where it turned and was soon out of sight heading off to the village.

Slowly, painfully, Walter made his way to the green, wooden benches at the bus stop and sat down. He stared across the road at the post office building, the pain in his leg almost forgotten, a postscript to what he'd witnessed. Another bus pulled in at the stop and he moved away so that others would not think him part of the queue. His mind was in turmoil. From what he'd seen Betty was married. He could come to no other conclusion. It was unthinkable but patently true. He'd seen her. He'd seen her with children. He sat down on a bench outside the bus station at the leg of one of the arches. He needed to think. He'd told himself and everyone at the convalescent home that he wanted to see family and friends, just to see them to make up his mind about how to contact them. But if the truth be told he only wanted to see Betty. It was only natural, but he'd convinced himself that she was secondary to his need to see his parents, and others, but it wasn't so. He'd travelled all this way to see Betty, and only Betty. But, and now the truth hit home, it was ten years since he'd left her. She hadn't wanted him to go. He could hear her now begging him to stay, he could see her tears and hear her sobs. He could smell her scented hair. But, he'd had to go! Everyone else was going, and he didn't want to be the only one to miss out. He thought it would be fun, a lark. Look at him now! He believed now that Betty thought he was dead. They all did. His parents, his brother and his wife, any children they may have. They all thought he was dead. The government had told them so. What good was it going to do anyone him suddenly arriving out of the blue? Look I'm here! I'm not dead! All the others who'd lost loved ones, whose loved ones had been killed, it would open all the old wounds. His parents would have to start to re-think their lives upon his return. What would they do? The shock; It would kill his mother, probably. There would be no work for him, what would he do? He would be alone. There would be resentment, no doubt. He'd seen it himself when men had come back to the home, unable to manage outside when they'd been given their jobs back at someone's expense, and then not been able to cope.

What about Betty? What would she think? What would she feel? She'd married, obviously thinking him dead. She'd feel guilty, she'd feel anger. She'd hate him for putting her through everything she'd been through, and then just turning up again wanting everything to be back the way it was. All this was his fault. He'd wanted to go to war, everyone argued against it, but he had to go.

He didn't want to lose the feelings he had for Betty. He would never lose them! Thinking about her had got him through all this. It was his own fault she wasn't his wife. She shouldn't feel guilty, he would hate it if she came to resent him; all his memories and all of hers would be tainted. No! He couldn't go home. It wouldn't be fair. He shouldn't just think about himself. He did want to go home. He did want to see his parents. But what good would it do to open up all these wounds, and at the end he would not have Betty. How could he? She was married. He could keep all his memories and she could keep all of hers; all good ones, only if he went back. He had a job, and he was reasonably happy at the home. The people there knew and understood him and his needs. That was the best thing to do for all concerned. He would go back, and think about what to write to his parents. That would be the best thing. A letter to pave the way. It would be wrong to just spring his return on them out of the blue. That's what Freddy had advised, and as usual he was right.

Having made his decision Walter was surprised to find that, by the bus station clock, he'd been sitting on the bench for almost two hours. He picked up his case and entered the terminus, passing a pot full of flowering roses on his way, and having to be careful not to kick the pigeons around his feet. He smiled noticing among the scavengers a few white doves. The sight of them brought a hint of sadness to his memories of Betty. Inside, to his frustration, he realised he'd forgotten his hat. He'd never worn a hat before and when he got back he would never wear one again he vowed, returning to the bench to retrieve it. He'd only brought it because Freddy had bought it for him. He'd be able to talk over his trip and his

166

decisions with Freddy upon his return. This thought made him feel better.

It was this return to the bench that allowed Dancy Prentiss to notice him.

Dancy had been to the main post office for a reprimand. Someone, no one knew who, had been talking about a certain family in the town, something that could only have been known by someone reading a postcard. The family had complained, citing an instance in the past where something similar had occurred. That postcard had been delivered by Dancy. Of course being a postcard meant anyone who'd handled it could have read it, but that wasn't the point as the postmaster made abundantly clear to Dancy at his interview. It was only the fact that the missive was a postcard that saved Dancy his job. He received a final warning and was told to be very careful in the future. Dancy was pleased to be outside the post office and still in work. It was on leaving the building, after the fraught meeting with his superior, that he happened to look across the road at the bus station opposite in general, and at the bench Walter had occupied, in particular. If Walter hadn't gone back for his hat Dancy would never have seen him. As it was, it was only Walter's limp, on his aching leg that, drew Dancy's attention to him. When he straightened up after retrieving the prodigal hat Dancy saw him. Walter turned and was gone into the shadows of the building in seconds but it was long enough for Dancy, who'd known Walter all his life, to recognise him. He crossed the road and went to the ticket barrier. He watched as Walter boarded the Nottingham bus, just to be sure his eyes had not deceived him. That night in the Globe, as Dancy recounted his story, he was ridiculed. No one believed him. Everyone in the bar laughed at him. They all laughed except Betty's ghosts. They said nothing, not even amongst themselves. Anyone watching them closely would have seen a momentary, glance pass between them. But the watcher would have had to have been watching very closely indeed.

That evening in Nottingham, Walter took a cheap hotel room near the railway station, and after he had dined on takeaway fish and chips eaten out of the paper, and washed down with a pint of the local brew, he went to bed. Here he tossed and turned, re-living the images of Betty and her family long into the dark stretches of the night. In the morning, after his ablutions and a shave in cold water from the water jug in his room, he left the hotel and caught the early train to London. He dozed as it steamed through the countryside towards the great metropolis, his restless night having left him tired and irritable. After a night in London he made his way back to the home in Hampshire. His mood hadn't changed for the better when he reached his destination, and after first visiting Freddy to ensure his return to work was noted he retired moodily to his room. Freddy thought it best to leave him alone accepting that his visit had been, to say the least, traumatic for him. Walter wasn't seen around the hospital for three days. After this time he re-appeared and it was as if nothing had happened. He seemed to be back to himself, and Freddy was pleased to see Walter back to normal.

Not long after Walter's return Freddy received a missive from the War Office, his paymasters. This told him that the home was to be re-branded as a Sanatorium for all, not just war wounded. Basically nothing changed but the name of the home, and Freddy's door was re-painted with a new sign bearing the legend Dr Pearce. But now the place would be allowed to take in patients from the local hospitals in need of convalescent care, which they had been doing, unbeknown to the powers that be for some time, in order to help out these institutions, which had long been under pressure.

Freddy was now able to have a large workshop built in the grounds where Walter would be able to work. He justified this expense by saying that Walter would be teaching other patients woodwork as a rehabilitation tool. This explanation was accepted and Walter was soon at work in the new workshop. Freddy noticed that since his return Walter had been much quieter than usual. He put this down to the chastening lesson he'd learned while he'd been away, and counted it no bad thing. He hoped that Walter, once he'd come to terms with his discoveries, would write to his parents and tell them what had happened to him. He was sure this was the path for Walter to take, but it had to be Walter's choice. No one could make him do it; he had to want to return to his family, with all that the return would mean for everyone concerned.

Once the new visitors to the newly named Sanatorium saw the dovecote Walter had built, with its calming birds using it, other institutions wanted them. The first was the local public house. The landlord, whose brother was in the sanatorium for respite care after a serious operation saw it and immediately asked where it was from. On learning that it had been built in-house he ordered one, and Walter was more than pleased to oblige him. Walter was pleased because by now he had more birds than his small cote could accommodate; so with each new dovecote he built he could also supply the inhabitants. Walter quickly built the new cote for the pub, with the help of some of his students from the wards. He set these men on shaping the timbers for the walls and painting the pieces as they were ready. This way the cote was much better waterproofed than his original ones. He also puttied up the joints of the timbers to the roof and cut thin laths to cover the joints which were also puttied into position; this made for a fully watertight roof. All these thing had been learned through experience, and now Walter was sure he was building dovecotes that would last for years.

The pub's dovecote was erected, to much fanfare by the landlord, who had the local newspaper there to take photographs and to write the story. He laid on a picnic outside his tavern for all-comers to mark the event, which went down very well with the locals, and the reporter, to judge by the glowing report he submitted and which was subsequently published. The local council, not to be out-done, decided they would have one erected on the village green outside the council offices, and so Walter's building work continued apace, and he seemed to have gotten over his trip north. He became more his normal self as time drifted by, and he immersed himself in his tutoring duties. Soon he had his students working on two projects at once, and he himself was just overseeing the work. Freddy looked upon this as a step in the right direction and was pleased with himself for thinking of the workshop idea, and bringing it to fruition.

While this was happening, Dancy, spurred on by the derision he had received in the pub from his friends when he said he'd seen Walter Blower, pondered on the conundrum while he delivered his letters. How could he prove what he'd most certainly seen? He wanted to keep the story running because it took the gossip away from his misdemeanour with the postcard; if people were talking about Walter they wouldn't be talking about himself. Finally, after days of consideration he came up with, in his mind, the perfect solution: he'd ask Mr. Blower! Dancy postulated that it was afternoon when he'd seen Walter (the memory of that reprimand interview, was burned into his memory, he would never forget the date; it still caused Dancy to blush with embarrassment); Walter was going back to where he'd come from. Therefore he'd already visited whoever it was he'd been to see. As his old girlfriend was now married with children he must have been visiting his parents. Therefore he'd ask them. Quite simple when you thought it through. He smiled to himself at the solution. No time like the present, he thought. From where he was now, in order to reach the Blower's, he had to detour by the gypsy camp and down the lane towards the cottages on the edge of the estate. Not far out of his way. He was lucky enough to catch sight of Walter's father as he passed through the gate from the estate onto the lane, gliding to a halt alongside him he asked the question.

At first Walter's father was stunned. He thought Dancy must have completely lost his mind. When Dancy realised he'd made a mistake he began to bluster, and through the bluster Walter's father gained the knowledge of what Dancy was talking about, and, reading between the lines, why it was so important to him. He gently chastised Dancy and made him understand how hurtful what he was saying was to himself and more to the point, to Mrs. Blower, who was still struggling with the loss. Dancy, at first, insisted he was not mistaken, and that he was positive that he had seen Walter in the town. Over the next half hour though Walter's father wore Dancy's resistance down, explaining that Dancy's logic was faulty.

If Walter was alive who would he travel to see first, but his parents? Dancy agreed, that was what he'd surmised. Now that Betty was married his first port of call would be his parents and then he would search out his friends, who would most probably be in the Globe public house. Was that not so? Dancy agreed it was. Who knew where Walter's friends would be? Everybody in the village. Dancy nodded. So, continued Mr. Blower, to a much chagrined Dancy, following his own reasoning, Walter would have visited the Globe after asking someone where his friends were, wouldn't he? Dancy now looking at his boots agreed. He could see where this argument was going. Had anyone else seen or spoken to

Walter? No! Had Walter been to the Globe? No! Had he visited his parents? No! So following Dancy's own logic to its ultimate conclusion. Had he seen Walter? No! Whoever it was he had seen, and no matter how much he looked like Walter, after all this passage of time, the person could not have been Walter. Could it? After this argument Dancy had to agree with Mr. Blower, it could not. Dancy apologised, not wanting to get into any more trouble, and cycled off. Still at the back of his mind he wondered as he pedalled away, who would look that much like Walter, whoever it was they'd caused him a great deal of trouble. He re-doubled his efforts over the pedals; he wanted to be far away from the cottages as quickly as possible. He wanted to leave this episode in his life far behind. He panted out onto the lane and headed back to the village, his mind whirling with Mr. Blowers words ringing in his ears.

As Walter's father made his way home he also had a lot to think about. He was pleased that he'd stopped Dancy spreading the rumour. He'd heard about the postcard incident and knew what Dancy had been about. He didn't want his wife hearing such things about Walter. Her mental state was very unstable where anything to do with Walter was concerned. The gypsy's intervention had caused him all sorts of problems over the years. She just would not accept that Walter was dead, and Dancy spreading such news would certainly have made her worse. He'd just managed, over the last couple of years, to get her back to something resembling normal to the outside world. He realised himself she could never be the same following the loss of Walter, and she continued to tend the roses in the garden with loving care, extending their flowering period for as long as she could, with dead-heading and wind shelters, which totally surrounded the bushes at the back end of their growing season. But he could cope with that. He just didn't want anything now that could upset her equilibrium. He could manage her as she was.

There were a couple of things that Dancy had said, that made him think though. Dancy did know Walter very well and he had known him all of his life. They had played together as children, and Dancy had made a lot of Walter; he'd loved him and called him his best friend, much to Walter's embarrassment. He shook his head as he pushed open the gate to his cottage. Don't let Dancy's nonsense into your head, he thought, or you'll end up as daft as he is. If, by any chance Walter is still alive he would get in touch, someway or other, wouldn't he? It would be the first thing he would do. Wouldn't it? He walked down the rose scented garden path and pushed open the cottage door; the enticing smell of meat and potato pie greeted him, and a kiss on the cheek from a loving wife. All was well with the world in the Blower household, for today, anyway.

***

As Dancy had been telling the men in the Globe that he'd seen Walter at the bus station, Betty and her family were travelling home on the bus. Betty was reflecting on the visit to her parents to celebrate the birthday of her oldest child, Walter. It had been a costly journey, what with the ever changing wages offered by the mine owners, always trying to raise production by lowering the wages to make the men work harder and longer. The look on her mother's face when she'd seen the four of them on the doorstep had made it worthwhile, and it was the same when her dad got home, his joy at seeing her and the boys had been almost overwhelming, and he really got on well with Matty, or Mathew as he insisted on calling him. With the children sleeping in their arms she and Matty had discussed trying to make the long journey more often. As Matty had said, her parents weren't getting any younger and the journey was an arduous one for themselves, it must be doubly so for her parents. She had enjoyed the day though and she smiled as she thought about it as she dozed with her head on Matty's shoulder, as they journeyed through the ever darkening night.

The walk home through the dark streets from the bus-stop, had given Betty time to reflect on Matty's parents. She would love to get to know them better but the journey to see them was even longer than the one they'd just undertaken, and as things stood they could never afford to make the long journey north.

Now, though, they were home and it was bedtime, and those thoughts were for another day. Tomorrow was bread-making day for her and back down the mine for Matty. She closed the cottage door and made a night-time cup of tea as Matty put the boys to bed. She smiled tiredly to herself as she poured the water over the tea leaves. It had been a good day all round for the Campbells.

CHAPTER EIGHTEEN.

In Hampshire Walter settled down to his solitary life, working and living at the sanatorium. His reputation as a carpenter was well known, but now his skills as an all-round handyman were beginning to spread and his time was being filled doing little tasks for the people who lived around the home, always providing, of course, that his tutoring skills weren't needed there. He replaced missing slates at one property and re-glazed a window at another, and at a third he replaced a garden gate. This job he incorporated into his tutoring work by letting his students make the gate, once he'd measured it up and discussed the style with the house owner. His life, to an outsider seemed to be going well. But at night, when he was alone Walter could think only of his life without Betty and how different it could have been but for one bad decision. During the day, when he was busy, he was able to keep these thoughts at bay, but in the evenings and at night, they infiltrated his mind to such an extent that he resorted to asking Freddy for a sleeping draught on odd occasions. Freddy obliged but he was worried about Walter, although he kept these feelings to himself, while, keeping a close eye on his favourite patient.

Dr George had visited Walter on a number of occasions over the years and these visits had always lifted Walter's spirits, but the visits recently had become fewer and fewer as the doctor's health had worsened. Old age was catching up with him and Freddy had received a letter from one of Dr George's colleagues telling his British friends to expect the worse, and not to rely on any more visits from Dr George as he was now very ill. Freddy had asked, by return post, to be kept informed about the good doctor's situation. By the time the answering letter arrived Dr George had died. Freddy contemplated telling Walter the bad news, but because of Walter's fluctuating mood swings, and his need for sleeping draughts, Freddy had decided against it. Freddy made the trip to Belgium alone for the funeral, citing work as an excuse when Walter had asked him about the trip.

Walter, many times, wrote out an envelope with his parents' address on it, but he could never bring himself to write the letter to go inside. Every time he tried he found some reason not to do it. He was too tired, it was too late; he didn't have enough ink of the right colour. He'd have to buy some black ink; he would disrupt his parent's lives for no good reason. But the truth of the matter was that he didn't want to go back without being able to see Betty. If he did turn up it would cause her pain, and he didn't want to do that. He had caused enough pain for everyone, especially Betty, and he didn't want to inflict any more. He knew deep down this was the reason, and he knew also that it was selfish; his parents would love to know that he was alive whatever upheaval it may cause, but he couldn't change the way he felt. So the letter remained unwritten.

Betty meanwhile was being kept busy; she had quite a business going making bread, and had, after picking blackberries which grew wild all along the hedgerows around where she lived, one day made some jam (another one of Audrey's recipes). She'd given a jar to Annie and it had been a big hit. Some of her bread customers had requested jars and she'd had the idea of making soups and jams to sell. In the winter just gone she'd given some soup to her customers while they waited, and that had gone down well too. She'd thought then of making soup to sell, but had been too busy with other things to think the idea through. Now though, along with the jam, she thought both together would be a good idea; she was in discussions with Matty about the project. He'd agreed it was a good idea, in principle, but had also pointed out that if they wanted to travel to see her parents more often, the money they had saved for the trip would be the money she would have to use to buy sugar and other ingredients for her jam. The blackberries came free, he agreed, she just had to pick them, but everything else cost money. He'd been right, of course, and she did want to see her parents again, but she hadn't quite given up on her idea just yet. She was sure she could find a way to do both things. She just had to work it out, before broaching the idea again.

Betty was feeling particularly pleased with herself. The poacher had been round and she'd managed to swop a jar of her jam for two pigeons. Matty loved pies and she thought a pigeon pie would be a nice change to the normal meat ones she made with the gristly meat from the local butcher. A pleasant surprise, she thought, after his long shift. She was humming a tune to herself, as she rolled out the pastry. The boys were both asleep in their bedroom so she had no distractions. Suddenly the air was rent with the sound of the pit siren. This was strange, she'd never heard the sound at this time of day before. Normally it was to call the men to work.

Betty went to the door, leaving her half prepared pie on the table. The road outside was full of people. Men in their shirtsleeves, some with the collars turned in as if caught having a wash or a shave. Some were half shaved. Some only in vests, despite the chill in the air. Women were dressed in their turbans and pinafores, some obviously coming from cleaning the range, or setting the fire. Others, like Betty covered in flour caught while baking. Betty could feel the tension in the air; every face in the quickly moving crowd was facing towards the pit-head. All looked grim. None looked at anyone else. Some of the women were running and openly crying. To Betty this was a new experience and she knew it was bad. Something was seriously wrong, and this was Matty's shift. She ran out into the street and, leaving her door open, as many around were, she joined the sombre crowd. She wiped her flour covered hands on her colourful, wrap around pinafore, and ran with the swiftly moving throng, wiping away tears as she moved. She didn't know why she was crying, but the atmosphere was such that it made her weep. She was frightened, fear tying her stomach in knots. The front of the crowd had now reached the gates which they found locked. Officials of the mining company stood as a group on the other side of the wrought iron gates which bore the company name in grimy gold lettering. Word passed back through the muttering crowd; the officials had told the front runners that there had been a fall. It was nothing to worry about, everyone was all right and the men were being dug out. It was on the Sherwood Heading. Betty heard the news. The Sherwood seam was where Matty was working. He'd been so pleased when he told her that he'd been moved. He said the coal was better there and there was more chance to make money on that seam. The siren stopped but no one moved. There were mutterings among the men in the crowd. Some of them didn't believe they were hearing the full story. Some began to push at the locked gates. The officials stepped back. They spoke amongst themselves and then two stepped forward and told the crowd to leave. No one moved. Time seemed to drag by. Betty looked around the sea of grim faces trying to see someone she knew, but there wasn't a face she recognised. If she could find someone she knew she would ask them what was happening. Maybe they'd been through this before and could help her understand.

The front of the crowd began to buzz with activity. Word carried back. The pit-head wheels were turning. She looked up at the spider-work of metal that carried the giant wheels which raised and lowered the cage carrying the men to and from their work every day. The buzz got louder. The officials tried to move the crowd back from the gates again, but to no avail. The front of the crowd could see blackened men leaving the building which housed the cage. The officials, looking grim, retreated again. One of the men, dressed in working clothes, who had come out of the pit-head building, came down, past the remonstrating officials, to the gates. An official tried to grab him as he passed but he roughly pushed him aside, smearing his suit coat with black dust. As the man approached the gates the crowd surged forward and the pit company men hastily retreated into their offices.

Firedamp! Firedamp! The words spread through the crowd like a plague. Firedamp! Firedamp! Betty desperately looked around for someone she knew to explain what it meant. Matty was still down there. What did this mean? As she desperately searched the crowd for a recognizable face, there was a rumble deep down in the earth. Everything stopped. It was as if time itself stood still. There wasn't a sound to be heard. Every face looked at every other face in the silent crowd. Then pandemonium broke out. The crowd surged forward and the locked gates buckled and flew open. The shouting crowd rushed in. The pit company men locked the office doors and hid away from the windows.

The crowd ran as one to the pit head. Suddenly the crowd halted. People ran into the back of the person in front. Some stumbled and fell, only to be grabbed and lifted upright by their neighbour. The crowd was silent again. A man, begrimed and sweating, stood in the doorway of the building which led to the shaft. He raised a hand, all movement stopped. Silence reigned. The silence of the graveyard.

"Today…" he began, his voice filled with emotion as he spoke. "Today, we had a fall on the Sherwood seam. It trapped the hewers and their mates. While we were digging them out there was a build-up of methane."

"Firedamp," someone whispered near Betty. Someone shushed the whisperer and the orator continued.

"We had to evacuate the area and before we all got out there was a small explosion. More roof gave way. We only just made it out. We've just felt the rest of the seam go. The men still below are going to seal off the heading to stop the fire which has broken out. Or we lose the pit." He stopped speaking. No one spoke. The speaker took a deep breath and continued, "We lost seven men. Their names are…"he began to read from a list he had on a grubby piece of paper he produced from his waistcoat pocket. The first name he read was Cecil Walker, the next name he read out was Mathew Campbell. Betty heard no more.

When Betty awoke she was in her own bed. Annie Clegg was in the room with her. "What happened?" Betty asked confused. Then realization dawned and she tried to rise.

"No girl. No." Annie spoke harshly, "Stay there. Drink this."

Betty shook her head, but Annie would brook no refusal and Betty was forced to drink the bittersweet liquid. "That'll make you sleep."

Betty began to protest, but Annie completely ignored her and began to tuck her in to her bed, tightly. "The youn 'uns are alright. You sleep."

Betty slept.

The following day the full horror of what had occurred hit her. She was one of seven new widows in the village. That was the truth at its starkest. Just the bare facts. No more Matty. No more daddy. Walter could say daddy now. But he didn't need to any more. His daddy was gone. Betty sank into a state at first of apathy. Annie and her friends rallied round, but couldn't drag Betty from the place she found herself in, and then she slipped even further away. Annie was forced to look after her in her bed; she feared what Betty may do to herself, and more to the point, to the boys. So for a time she separated them. During this time she forced Betty to listen to what she said, at times violently shaking her, to get and keep her attention. But she made Betty listen.

"Matty lives in those lads. Don't you forget that. Ever." Annie kept repeating to her, and Betty knew what Annie said was true. But how could she go on now, after this? She had to pull herself together. But could she? First Walter, now Matty. She raved and ranted in her shock. She cried, screaming out in her agony so much that at times Annie felt sure she was slipping into lunacy. Betty had never felt such pain, such loss. It was as though she were cursed. She said as much to Annie in the depths of her despair. Annie looked at her with disdain, "I thought you had more about you than that," she said before closing the bedroom door. In one of her more lucid moment she knew that Annie, in her gruff way was right. She had no option but to carry on if only for the boys. Annie's abrupt manner and harsh words, had shocked Betty, but it gave her the stimulus she needed to start to pull herself round, and with the ministrations of her friends, particularly Annie, she began to recover. When she did she was a different person to the girl who had arrived just a couple of short years ago at the mining village. She was harder, wiser and more self-contained. Betty had come out of her shock a stronger person. Annie liked who she'd become. Betty thought back to the day of the disaster and cringed at what she'd done.

She'd run out of the house when she'd heard the siren and left the boys alone. Luckily they'd been fast asleep and the siren hadn't woken them. Annie had found them and looked after them until now. Now she must think of them. She couldn't thank Annie enough. Annie waved her thanks away, "Nothing to thank me for. Just watch over them lads. That's thanks enough," she said.

The boys helped her to struggle through the grief. Through the funerals. As with the war, she thought, a funeral without a body. Seven funerals and then a memorial service. The memorial service was attended, by the entire workforce, and colliers from all the surrounding pits. The mine was closed that day, much to the disgust of the mine owner.

Just when she thought she was over the worst she found out that she would have to vacate the cottage as it was needed for one of the new miners and his family who would be taking over from the seven lost men. Her despair was almost palpable. She was not only a widow with two boys, now she was homeless too.

Betty gave Annie her few sticks of furniture to dispose of as she thought fit, and with what she could carry she made her way back to her mother's cottage, promising to keep in touch with Annie no matter what.

CHAPTER NINETEEN.

Her mother and father were glad to have her home although in the tiny cottage it was a crush with the two growing boys. Betty had discussed the move at Matty's funeral, but then she thought she would have time to find a place to live, and a job of her own as she would have to find work to provide some income now, to support the three of them. She never intended putting her mother and father into such a predicament as they were in now. The adults all knew that the situation couldn't last but the boys loved every minute of it. Especially when granddad took them to meet Polly, his Shire horse in the forest.

With help from the Cohens, Betty soon found lodgings for herself and the boys. Three rooms, but it would do for the time being. It also gave her parents their home back. The laundry was only too pleased to welcome her back into her old job. She had applied with some trepidation. Remembering her problems the last time she'd worked there with Joan Lowes, but, Mrs Lowes had left their employment under a cloud, so Betty didn't have to worry about her, and her bullying attitude. No one ever spoke about her, or what had caused her to leave; everyone from Betty's, earlier time at the laundry knew of the bad blood between the two, so no one spoke of her in Betty's presence. It was as if she had never existed, which suited Betty in her present frame of mind, down to the ground. Betty soon got back into the swing of things and with the help of her friends her fortunes seemed to pick up. Her mother and Mrs. Cohen bickered, constantly but good naturedly, about who was looking after the two boys, who were spoiled, by their ever growing family of aunts and uncles. Especially when Betty rekindled her friendship with Audrey and everyone from the Manor, which was when aunties Dora, Jenny, Audrey, and not forgetting the Burtons came into their lives.

It was 1926 and the General Strike. Because of the intransigence of the mine owners, wanting men to work underground, longer hours for less pay, bringing into being the mineworkers famous slogan 'Not a penny off the pay, not a minute on the day. The TUC voted to back the miners action, and so on Tuesday the fourth of May the General Strike began. Only nine days later though, the TUC, believing the government negotiators, called off the action. The government's words proved to be spurious but the General Strike was over. The miners continued to fight on alone, but after six months were forced by poverty to go back to work. The miners had lost!

Betty felt for them, knowing what it was like to be a miner's wife first hand, and knowing how dangerous the work was. But she had known that the strike was a futile gesture, when it began. She understood that the miners had been pushed beyond endurance and even when the whole country seemed to support them, she knew first hand, how strong the mine owners were. Nine days later, when the strike crumbled, she hated herself for being right. The miners were now in a worse position than they had been before the strike.

But she had her own problems; worrying about the miners wouldn't help her boys. They were her priority, and they were growing rapidly now. She concentrated all her efforts into bringing up her sons, other people's problems didn't concern her. 1926 was the year Walter started school, so the year wasn't all bad. Betty managed to get him a place at Maid Marian Primary School, which was just down the road from her parents' house. Walter loved it, after a rocky initial start, and because his mother was working, he had his dinner every day at his grandmother's, which he loved even more, as she fed him whatever he asked for. Within reason.

He enjoyed his school milk, at ten o'clock playtime, for which Betty paid one penny per day. She felt this was well worth it. Walter soon made friends and these friendships soon involved Edward too. Edward shared his time between Mrs. Cohen and his grandmother; Mrs. Cohen used Walter having his dinner at his grandmothers ruthlessly in order to keep looking after Edward. Saying she was helping out and giving Betty's mum more time to do her own work. Everyone knew what was happening and was willing to play along. She just loved the boys, and having no children of her own would do anything to look after them. The boys loved it all, as they were the centre of attention wherever they went. Betty was happy with the way things were now going, and it paid testament to her parenting skills that the boys were growing up so level-headed amidst all the attention they received.

Things got even better for them when her landlady told her she had a cottage coming up for rent. The old lady who lived there was moving out to live with her son who was able to look after her now, as his own son had married and left home, making room for her. So, as Mrs. Cohen had put in a word for Betty, she thought the place would suit her. It would take a little putting right as the old lady hadn't done much to it. But if Betty accepted it, she could pay the first six month's rent at the same cost as she paid for her rooms. After that they would discuss the rent again. Betty accepted without even seeing the place. She trusted her landlady as a friend of Mrs Cohen's and her trust was not misplaced. The cottage was a little run down but nothing Betty couldn't handle and it was closer to her mother's and Walter's school. Betty was ecstatic. A place of her own; she rushed off to tell her mam.

During talks with Audrey, when she took the boys to see her at the Manor, Betty had discussed her thwarted plans for selling soups and jams. Audrey had said what a good idea she thought it was and the two old friends decided to give it a try. With the help of Mrs. Cohen they began to sell their produce around the fairs and although they made a small profit they both knew that it was the companionship they both craved, just having someone to talk to, and confide in. During one of these days at the fair, business had been quiet and the three women were standing together on the coconut shy talking about making a cup of tea when a customer arrived at Mrs Cohen's jewellery stall. She bustled off leaving Audrey and Betty together. Out of the blue Audrey said, "I was too young when I married Duncan. I never should have done it." Betty had never heard Audrey speak about her marriage before. Audrey had always been a very private person and had never spoken to anyone about her own life before the Manor. Betty kept quiet and Audrey, looking far off into the distance, continued, "Remember how you got with Walter, wanting to be married, not wanting to wait."

Betty nodded, but wasn't sure Audrey noticed.

"I was worse than that. I had no one to advise me. I'd been brought up in an orphanage you see. That's where I learned to cook, in the orphanage kitchens. Duncan was a soldier; there were barracks nearby, and we started walking out. Before long we were talking about getting married. I didn't know what that entailed. I'd never ever thought someone like me would get married. Anyway Duncan got permission and that was that. I think I was fifteen, I might have been younger. I never really knew how old I was. We had three months together and then he went off to Africa. We were fighting the Boers then. I thought I'd be going with him, but apparently it wasn't allowed. Next thing I knew, I'd got the letter. He was killed in action. That was that." She stopped speaking and just stood there, leaning on the post which carried the green and red striped awning, which covered the shy. "Pregnant and a widow. A soldier's wife. Who'd be one?" She concluded.

Betty made a move towards her but she seemed to shake herself out of her reverie and said, "This isn't selling any jam is it?" and she walked back onto their own stall. That was the one and only time Audrey ever spoke of her past, as far as Betty knew. She felt privileged to have been given this glimpse into her friend's life. Even if it was so enigmatic. She would have loved to learn more, but knew if she questioned Audrey that was the surest way to make her stop talking. The only way was to let Audrey speak in her own time. As things turned out it didn't matter, she never opened up again.

It was during one of her visits to the Manor to see Audrey that the boys met Mr. Blower. They'd been running around outside the kitchen when the two women noticed how quiet it had become. When they went to the door to see what the boys were up to they were nowhere to be seen. When they both began to shout the boy's names, Walter appeared at the garden gate closely followed by Mr Blower. Betty left Audrey on the kitchen steps, and dreading the confrontation went to meet him. She needn't have feared, he was pleased to see her and gave her a hug, much to the amusement of her sons. When she tried to explain, how she'd been meaning to bring the boys to see him, but was worried about the effect it would have on Mrs. Blower, he quietened her with a wave of his hand and told her that he understood. He told her how much he appreciated her thoughtfulness, both for thinking about his wife and for naming the boy Walter. There were a few tears on both sides. The embarrassed boys, searched through the greenhouses for the toads Mr Blower had been about to show them before their mother arrived, while the emotive meeting finished.

When they parted he asked her not to let the boys meet his wife, but hoped on any further visits he could see them, which she assured him he could. The boys were pleased, having discovered one of the toads, and knowing they would get the opportunity next visit, to find more. They were also promised a visit to the dovecote. Betty questioned him about that expecting, after all this time, for it to have fallen into disuse. Mr. Blower pointed to some birds circling in the sky and a couple of the fantailed doves canoodling on the roof. "More eggs on the way I shouldn't wonder." He laughed. "I've kept up with the maintenance Betty. Not up to Walter's standards I know. But it's still there. Them birds you see, they're the offspring of the ones Walter put in. Third maybe fourth generation. It'll be there as long as I'm able to look after it." Betty declined to see it, as Mr. Blower knew she would. Too many memories for her.

Audrey and Betty were both pleased with the way things had turned out, although Audrey always thought it would work out well, knowing the sort of man Mr. Blower was.

Betty's life at that time, seemed to be a kaleidoscope of happenings when she sat and thought about it in later life. One thing seemed over and suddenly there was something else happening. It didn't give her time to dwell on anything, which she felt was a good thing at the time.

Time drifted by and soon Edward was at school with Walter. Betty was enjoying her time on the fairs with Audrey and they were now fast friends; after Audrey's earlier revelations the two had grown ever closer. Betty kept her promise to Annie, visiting her as often as she could and on occasions taking the boys along, which was as great a treat for them as it was for Annie. Naomi took Betty to see her in-laws in Durham with the boys in her car, whenever she could, and as Betty got to know them better so they became good friends with Naomi. They made the trip down to see their grandchildren as often as monetary restraint would allow.

Suddenly, it seemed to Betty, Walter was fourteen and leaving school. Where had the time gone? He found work in the forest with his grandfather, which suited him perfectly, him being at home in all pursuits which kept him outdoors. He'd grown into a fine strapping lad, the image of his father. Betty was really proud of him. She noticed a couple of the local girls always seemed to be around when Walter was home, and they seemed to follow whenever he and Edward went out together. She'd never really thought about either of her sons from the perspective of the local girls. But now, after noticing Walter's admirers, for she was sure it was Walter they were interested in, she looked at them with different eyes. She mentioned it to Mrs. Cohen and Audrey, one day in passing as they worked on the stalls. The two older women looked knowingly at each other and smiled. "You must be blind, our Betty," laughed Mrs. Cohen. She could hear Audrey chortling behind her. "You've a pair of heartbreakers there an' no mistake. Open your eyes. You're going to have half the village girls on your doorstep if you're not careful."

Betty blushed and looked at her two friends. They both nodded, "They're grown Betty. Best get used to it," nodded Audrey sagely. Mrs. Cohen agreed.

Betty had never thought about her sons as men before. They were still her little boys. It made her feel sad, in a strange, proud unexplainable way. Another rite of passage, had passed almost without her noticing it.

The following year it was Edward's turn to leave. The quiet one. He was the polar opposite of Walter, and didn't want to work outdoors, but because of the time he'd spent with the Cohens, he was able to procure a place with Mr. Cohen in his workshop, and was soon designing jewellery which Mr. Cohen proudly announced rivalled his own. Edward had always been the artistic one and now Mr. Cohen was putting that artistry to good use.

Betty was proud of both her boys, her only regret was that Matty had not been able to see how well they'd done. She was sure that wherever he was he would look down on them and be as proud as she was herself.

CHAPTER TWENTY.

When Walter left school in 1935 conscription had already been reintroduced in Germany and in 1936, the year Edward left, Hitler reoccupied the Rhineland. Betty tried not to listen to the wireless. Mr. Burton had purchased one for Audrey which took pride of place in the kitchen. It had its own table near the door leading out onto the passageway; she said it didn't like the draught from the outside door, which made everyone laugh, but Betty, who knew Audrey better than anyone now, always thought she wasn't kidding. The wireless was in a large polished wood cabinet. It had a circular hole in the front with a gold grill over it which hid the speaker. The cabinet itself was shaped like an ornamental arch, pointed at the top sloping gently down to a shoulder and then straight down to a wide base. Midway between the circular grill and the foot of the base were three knobs, and just above the knobs, was a piece of glass coloured brown, and on this was written in cream, the stations that could be used by turning the end knob. Audrey always chose the home service. This was where she heard all the news. The other knobs were on and off. Every time Betty visited Audrey now the wireless was on. Betty thought it was good company for Audrey but the problem was that Audrey knew all the news and enjoyed telling anyone who'd listen what was happening in the outside world, and Betty didn't always want to know.

On the eleventh of March 1938 Hitler annexed Austria and in September Czechoslovakia was dismembered by the Munich Agreement. In March of the following year Hitler occupied Czechoslovakia. March of the same year Hitler annexed Memel. It was only then that Neville Chamberlain promised British support for Poland. Betty learned all this from Audrey on her visits to the Manor. Audrey loved spreading the news; it seemed to Betty, that she didn't realise what it could mean. Because it came out of the wireless it appeared Audrey didn't think it was real. All Betty could think, was surely, they're not going to let it happen again.

On the first of September 1939 Hitler invaded Poland and on the third of September, Audrey informed anyone who would listen that we were at war with Germany.

Walter immediately wanted to join up. Betty, her world crumbling around her now, was frantic in her efforts to stop him. All she could see was another Walter, so many years ago leaving her for another war, never to return. It was only calming words from her father that soothed the situation. Walter still harboured ambitions to join the Army, but for the moment, he kept these to himself.

Dunkirk. Betty hoped that the news from here would quell Walter's will to join up. But it had the opposite effect. It made him more determined. But for the moment he said nothing.

***

In Hampshire, the Sanatorium had once again become a War Office hospital for injured servicemen. Soldiers rescued from the beaches, injured in mind and body once again filled the beds. Freddy, thought that working with the injured as a porter/orderly would be good therapy for Walter, now that he seemed fully cured, having not needed any medication for almost a year. Walter had been functioning extremely well within the confines of the Sanatorium; Freddy seconded him to the wards. He thought that the handyman would be more use there. And so it proved; at first.

Soon Walter didn't have enough hours in the day to fulfil his duties. The injured kept arriving. One of Walter's tasks was to document their injuries and to try to find out names, ranks and companies. Where they came from was of paramount importance when trying to relocate them nearer to their loved ones. It was this part of the job that began to take its toll on Walter. At first, much to Freddy's pleasure, he seemed to be coping well. He was fine when he was talking to the men, moving them around the hospital, which after so many years there, he knew like the back of his hand. Even taking them to the operating theatres, some with horrific injuries, didn't seem to worry him. Freddy would talk to him after his day's work and Walter would seem fine. He assured Freddy that he was sleeping well, in fact he joked, "Too well. I have difficulty getting out of bed I'm so tired some nights." They had both laughed.

His problems began in a small way at first. He became unable to rest. No matter how tired he was, it took him ages to get off to sleep. He didn't tell Freddy because he knew how busy everyone was. And he didn't want to trouble him. So it continued. Walter became more and more tired, and then the nightmares began, reliving times he'd thought long gone. He would wake, as he had once before with the sheets wringing wet, and his body soaked in sweat, his hands scrabbling for a non-existent gas mask, gasping for breath, the smell of chlorine stinging his nostrils. Walter determined to fight his problem. He'd been doing so well, everyone had said so. He would master this problem without bothering anyone. He was confident he could do it. So he kept his own counsel and continued with his work. To all intents and purposes he was functioning well. Everyone was proud of him, but they were all as tired as he was and no one saw the cracks appearing.

***

Back in the village, Betty witnessed the exodus of young men she hoped she would never have to see again. Just twenty-one years after the first time it was happening again. She couldn't believe it. Now the dreaded wireless told them Italy had joined the war on the German side and invaded Greece. Where would it end?

1941 was not a good year for the allies. Germany took over Yugoslavia and Greece was defeated. Towards the end of that year Italy and Germany declared war on the USA. Things were going from bad to worse. On the wireless the news was all about the Allied losses and the wounded. The newscaster tried to make the news sound as upbeat as he could but there was no disguising what he was saying. The Allies were losing this war.

On the Friday after Betty had heard the broadcast, Walter came home from work and told her he'd joined up. He'd gone with a group of lads from the village and they'd all done the same. She staggered back as if he'd physically struck her, and he had to catch her to stop her falling to the stone flagged kitchen floor. The feeling of déjà vu sent Betty reeling, her head spun. This couldn't be happening. Her strong front evaporated, this was her son. She begged with him, pleading on bended knee for him to reconsider. But he was adamant. His reasoning was that sooner or later he'd be conscripted. There'd already been some officials in the forest to the logging camp. If he volunteered he would be better paid, and able to decide himself where he wanted to go, by which he meant which company he served with. He wanted to join the Royal Electrical and Mechanical Engineers (R.E.M.E.) He thought he could do well there. She couldn't argue, but that same sense of dread and foreboding she'd felt once before many years ago for a different Walter, filled her soul. It was all happening again.

A week later he, and his friends were off to training camp. Betty watched the smiling faces disappear as she had once before. Walter completed his training and came home on embarkation leave at the end of September 1941. He laughingly said he didn't know where he was going, but he would write. He said goodbye to a house full of well-wishers. All four of his grandparents, Audrey, Dora, Jenny, the Cohens and the Burtons all came to wish him well. Betty held him at the gate until she could feel him squirming in her arms with embarrassment, as his uniformed friends all waited. But she didn't care. Finally she let him go to cheers from his friends. Walter couldn't understand what the fuss was about. He waved goodbye from the back of the truck, his face glowing red, as another Walter had done just a few short years ago. Betty couldn't get either image out of her mind for a long time after everyone had left. The two images merged in her mind forming one terrible picture. A thought she found hard to shake. Betty changed that day. She didn't notice it herself but all those close to her noticed a reticence about her, a fear of feeling happy, as if to be happy was to tempt fate.

Betty purposely began to rely on Edward more and more, finding things she needed his help with, that before Walter's leaving, she would easily have managed on her own. Subconsciously she hoped that this reliance would keep him at home. She hoped he would accept this extra responsibility, as man of the house, and that it would take his mind off the thoughts he had of joining his brother. She knew he and Walter had talked about this before Walter had left. The two boys were close and had always been together, she dreaded the thought of Edward joining up too. It was at times like this that she missed Matty the most.

Walter's leaving had brought thoughts of Matty back to the forefront of her mind. She tried not to dwell on his loss. She knew people thought that his death had made her a harder person, because she never spoke of him. But this was not the case. She talked of him to her sons all the time, and she thought of him, as Annie had suggested, as living on in them. She had found thinking of Matty in this way had helped her come to terms with his loss. She could see him in their mannerisms. In the turn of Edward's head, when she called to him, and in Walter's gait. She couldn't bear to think of losing him again through the loss of her sons. Could life be so cruel? But Walter's leaving had brought all these thoughts back and she was finding it difficult to cope.

Then came the bitterest blow. January 1942 saw Edward enlist. This, although Betty knew it was inevitable, broke Betty's heart. She was certain now that she had lost both her sons. She could see no way back. Edward joined the R.E.M.E. as had his brother. He did this in the hope that one day they would meet up and be able to work together. This didn't happen.

Edward had a similar send off to Walter's, except Matty's parents couldn't make it. Matty's father was seriously ill; dust, as they were told, a miners disease, and he had passed away before Edward had finished his basic training. Mrs Cohen took Betty to the funeral. It seemed to Betty that she was losing all ties with Matty at once. The funeral reminded her of the memorial service she'd attended for Matty; all Matty's family were colliers, and so the atmosphere at the service was very similar, a feeling of the inevitability of it all. Betty took this to be a harbinger of what was to come. She was glad when it was over and she could leave. The feeling though, stayed with her. The journey home was sombre and in the end Mrs. Cohen stopped trying to make conversation and the journey ended in companionable silence.

When Betty returned from the funeral, she found the house cold, quiet and empty. She felt lonely and dreaded every knock at the door. She began working in the house every minute she had to spare, in order not to think about her boys. She tried to always be busy. She patched cracks in the walls, and tried to seal draughty windows using putty. She continually cleaned out the fire and scrubbed the steps front and rear with white stone. Audrey heard of this mania and called to see her on a regular basis, hoping that her visits would help to calm Betty down. Finally she convinced her to come to the Manor and give her a hand there. This did help, and when they began to find their old routine, Betty slowly began to open up, and talk. She told Audrey, that she'd stopped going to see the Cohens and her parents as often as she used to, because it reminded her too much of her boys. In deference to Betty, Audrey left the wireless switched off when she was there. It was on one of these days at the Manor that Mr. Burton made Betty a proposition that she readily accepted.

The Manor had become a dormitory for fifteen girls of the land army. The girls worked on both estates, the Villiers's and the Major's. They were invaluable to both, but it was getting a bit much for Audrey, although she would never admit it, to cook and bake for them all the time. Now, as there was so much to do around both estates, there was talk of bringing in more girls, so he, as manager, thought it appropriate to get help for Audrey, and as Betty was used to the work and knew Audrey he thought it best to ask her first. If Betty accepted, he said he would have a word at the laundry for her, as the work would be classed as helping the war effort and, she would be able to go back to her job there, after the war, if she so wished. Betty was overjoyed, and acquiesced without a second thought. She was back at the Manor, doing a job she loved, with the people she loved. There was nothing to think about.

The job took her mind away from the horrors the solitude of her own empty home brought, and soon she was embroiled in the day to day life of the estate. She helped Mr Blower in the garden when she had time, but mostly she was busy in the kitchen, much as she had been when she first arrived so many years before. Walter's father, having heard the news about Betty's boys joining up found it hard at first to know what to say to her, but they were close enough for Betty just to squeeze his work-worn hand and let him know that she understood. After that moment things were as they should be, the unspoken words between them had been said loudly enough. Her life now had come full circle.

Since the departure of the Major's wife the Manor had become a little run down. She had never returned to the place, finding life in the metropolis more to her liking. Occasionally she would write to Mr. Burton about some trivial estate matter but mainly, now, she was a silent partner in the enterprise. As long as things ran smoothly, which Mr. Burton ensured they did, she was happy. The letter advising that the land girls should be billeted there had come as a surprise. Mr. Burton had had no prior warning of its happening, but the letter came from a management company rather than the woman herself so he wasn't really surprised. He'd had dealings with the company before and it seemed to him now that they were taking on more and more of the work she would normally have done herself. She seemed to be slowly releasing her grip on the estate. This gave Mr. Burton some cause for concern but at the moment he had other things on his mind. The only stipulation in the letter from the Major's wife was that the girls were to be kept on the ground floor. No one was to go upstairs. So the ballroom, which, when Betty first came to the Manor was where all the gala dinners were held, was turned into a dormitory. Audrey and Betty laid on buffet style meals for the girls, not knowing whether they would all be in together or not. It depended on what they were doing and where. With the buffet the girls could help themselves. The cooks were judged on results by the girls, and as there was never anything left over they both felt they were doing a good job. They were a motley crew, but on the whole they were a good set of girls. Mr. Burton never had any cause to complain about their work.

The girls paired up and took it in turns helping with the washing up. Betty met them all at one time or another, when they were over the kitchen sink washing, or at the draining board drying and it helped Betty talking to them. Most of them had loved ones away fighting. Husbands, lovers, brothers, that seemed to be the main reason they were there. They felt they were doing their bit to help their men and to bring them home as quickly as possible. Betty noticed how young they all looked. It made her feel quite old.

The girls would ask to listen to the wireless in the evenings before bedtime, and Betty, knowing why Audrey had turned it off switched it back on. Together they would all sit around listening to the broadcasts as the evening drew into night. Some of the girls would smoke, and others would chew gum, a pastime Audrey abhorred. She blamed the Hollywood cinema films for the spread of this habit, and refused to go to see them. After a time Betty got used to the broadcasts and the wireless was left on in the kitchen most of the time. At last it became just a background hum during the day as they worked. But subliminally, as the war dragged on, the news was getting through, most of it bad.

There was some elation when America joined the allies after the Pearl Harbour attack by the Japanese on December the seventh 1941. The American congress voted on December the eighth to join the Allies with one dissenting voice, that of Jeanette Rankin, a Republican representing Montana; she had been a life-long pacifist and stood by her beliefs; having also voted against joining in WW1. The elation was short lived as the news from the front seemed unrelentingly bad as the turn of the year took the war into 1942.

***

1942 became 1943 and one day at last some good news came from Audrey's wireless. It was May and the broadcaster was saying that all axis forces in North Africa had surrendered to the Allies. When Audrey told the girls at dinner that night there was a great whoop of joy and much dancing and celebration up and down the former ballroom. Not enough dancing to let the food get cold though.

That was the turning point, or so it seemed to Betty. In September, after the conquest of Sicily, the Allies landed in Italy, and Italy surrendered. On the thirteenth of October, Italy declared war on Germany. More dining room celebrations. 1944. June the sixth. The D Day landings. It seemed to the girls that there were battles all over Europe, according to the wireless. It was difficult to keep up with the news from the broadcasts. The wireless was a constant barrage of facts and figures about the war. All the girls wanted to know was who was winning, and eventually the news came over the airwaves that the Allies had the upper hand. More dancing, and this time the food nearly became cold. That was because of the pillow fight. Betty now began to harbour thoughts, buried deep in her psyche, that maybe her boys would come home safe to her after all. She didn't dare voice these thoughts but she did begin to hope all the same.

Betty was away from the village and her house for long periods. The dormitory was home to twenty-five girls now; as harvesting was about to begin, extra girls had been drafted in. The summer had been good and as a consequence a lot of the corn was ripening early as the end of July approached.

Being away Betty had missed seeing Dancy delivering his telegrams, but now he came to the Manor with one for her. Walter was listed missing, presumed killed on the D. Day landings. Betty was inconsolable. Her life truly had come full circle. There were many in the nearby town who lost men on the day of the landings or just after. Dancy was kept busy after June 1944 and into July as the death toll mounted and the casualties were able to be named.

For a long time after the news was delivered Audrey kept a close eye on Betty. She seemed to be running on automatic pilot. She did her work but it was as if she was elsewhere. Audrey, carefully at first, but later with more vigour reminded her that she had another son, and to think of him. Slowly, after the memorial service had been held, Audrey finally got through and Betty admitted, in a private moment that she had been grieving for two Walters. The loss of her eldest boy had brought everything back again. Her working at the Manor had not helped, it had magnified her loss. Audrey said she understood but still kept a quiet eye on her.

1945. April. Dancy arrived with another telegram for Betty. She tried to run from him but fainted away on the kitchen steps. It was Audrey that opened the envelope after she'd shooed Dancy away, stopping him from trying to pick Betty up. He cycled off much chastened.

"Betty. Betty." She felt a sharp smack across her face and a sickly, sour smell in her nostrils. She coughed, and pushed the smelling salts away. Dora was wielding the bottle. She was lying on the kitchen floor her head on pillows taken from the girls' dormitory. Audrey, with Dora's help, had managed to carry her inside, from the kitchen steps. "Betty. It's Edward. He's coming home."

She swooned again. Dora stepped in and woke her up a second time.

"What's happened? Is it all over?" Betty was at a loss. She pushed Dora away with her bottle. "I'm awake, Dora," she said sharply. Dora grinned, putting the cap back on the bottle, but keeping it in her hand. Just in case.

"Here. Read for yourself." Audrey passed the all-white envelope and its contents to Betty. It explained that Corporal Edward Kenneth Campbell had been wounded in action; it didn't say in which theatre he'd been engaged, but it did give date and time. It continued that the wounds were severe enough to warrant repatriation. The wounds were not life threatening. Corporal Campbell was in a hospital in Hampshire where he was convalescing and should be home by, and it gave a date, which was two weeks away.

Betty couldn't contain herself. She completely broke down. All the years of pent up emotions were released, she lay on the floor and wept. Sobbing like a child. She wept for a lost son, and a lost husband. A lost lover and for a son injured but returning to her. The complex emotions which shook her body were almost too much to bear. She couldn't take in everything she was feeling. It was too much for her to comprehend. She just cried until there were no more tears left. Then she sobbed, a dry hacking sound, worse than the weeping.

Audrey wept at Betty's distress. She wept for her loss but also in relief that at least she had one son coming home. Dora began to cry because the other two were crying. Although Jenny always said later, when she found the three of them, on the floor in floods of tears, holding each other that she thought Dora was only crying because she'd spilt the smelling salts.

Jenny made a cup of tea while everyone composed themselves: Betty apologising profusely for making a fool of herself; the others dismissing her apologies as unnecessary. The tea was poured and Jenny was brought up to date, which caused more tears. But everyone calmed down and a discussion was entered into about Edward's injuries. Everyone was worried as to the extent of them. "At least he's home," said Dora. Everyone nodded and a second cup was poured.

For the first time in, she couldn't remember how long, Betty felt relieved. It was a strange feeling for her to have. She realised this, but there was no other way to describe how she felt. Edward was home, and the way the war was going according to the news broadcasts it seemed he would not be going back. The war was almost won, if the wireless was to be believed, and so it proved to be.

Germany unconditionally surrendered all of its forces on the seventh of May 1945. By then Edward was home. He'd been hit by a small piece of shrapnel while in charge of a group of men trying to build a pontoon bridge across the Rhine. The shrapnel had caused damage to his back and shoulder. He'd been evacuated first to a field hospital and the he'd been taken by hospital ship to Dover. From there he'd gone to a little hospital in Hampshire where he'd been able to recuperate before being allowed home. He didn't know about Walter. Betty broke the news to him, which set him back somewhat. He told her he had an inkling that something had happened to him because they'd written to each other throughout the conflict and Walter's letters had stopped arriving some while ago. He feared the worst then, but hoped he was somewhere he couldn't communicate from. It was not to be. So Edward's homecoming was leavened with sadness. Betty was just pleased to have him back.

Edward quickly gained weight. He had been sadly undernourished on his return, according to Audrey, and so, much to the land girls' delight, and Edward's too, he ate with them whenever he was at the Manor, which was often, as Betty hated to have him out of her sight.

Edward had to go to the local hospital for regular check-ups and physiotherapy on his arm and hand but other than those minor inconveniences he was a free agent. One day in mid-July he received a letter from the M.O.D. which Dancy delivered to the Manor, warily, after his last performance, because he knew Edward would be with his mother there. The letter was good news, so Dancy needn't have worried. It contained Edward's demobilisation papers. For Edward Campbell the war was now officially over. This was cause for great celebration among the family and at the Manor.

As was the election of a Labour government on the twenty-sixth of July.

Edward's recuperation was now well under way and he was soon back at work with Mr. Cohen. He still had some problems with his grip. It was the right arm that had been damaged, but soon the dexterity was back, and he was able, almost, to do the intricate work he used to enjoy so much before he went away. Mr. Cohen and Edward would talk amiably as they worked together, both squinting through their respective magnifying glasses as they cut and soldered away at the jewellery. They talked about every subject under the sun, but Edward would never talk about the war. Mr. Cohen never broached the subject and Edward never mentioned it ever. It was over and that was enough for both of them.

Betty, her pleasure at Edward's return forever tinged with sadness, would watch him as he limped around the cottage or down the path to her mother and father's house. He used a stick because the damage to his back had left him weakened on the right side; he insisted that one day he would be rid of it, but it didn't matter to Betty whether he did or not, he was home and safe, that was all that mattered to her.

All over the country men were coming home and there was a feeling that things were getting back to normal.

Whatever normal was after such a long and terrible time. There was a new government with new ideas and a promise of better things to come. "We'll see," said Betty one day as they were discussing a wireless programme from the previous day. It was marvellous how the box on the kitchen table had begun to feature in nearly every conversation they had. Now it was generally the spur to any discussion.

Betty had stayed on at the Manor to help out while the girls were still there. There was still a lot of work to be done around both estates, and some of the girls had become enamoured of some of the local men and were in no particular hurry to leave. So Betty stayed on. It was good for her to have friends around as she still had some bad nights, even with Edward safe, and she knew whenever she felt down Audrey would always be there to help.

***

In Hampshire things were very different for Walter. At the hospital the men who were left after the initial rush of casualties, were the most badly damaged. A lot of them with no physical injuries at all. In these men Walter could see himself. More and more often now his nightmares returned. He knew he should go to Freddy for help, but he'd left it for so long he knew there would be repercussions and recriminations, as he was now he could not face a berating from his friend. So he struggled on.

Freddy had been concerned for some time about Walter. Unbeknown to Walter, Freddy had noticed his deterioration and was waiting for Walter to come to him. He wanted the lead to come from him because he thought that this would be the final step in his total recovery. Freddy thought that for Walter to understand that there would be times when he relapsed, and that this was a hurdle that could be overcome, would be the ultimate step on his road to recovery. Freddy felt Walter was almost there. He just needed to take this final step.

Walter's mental condition worsened until Freddy realised that he wasn't going to come for help, and stepped in. After some arguments he gave him a sedative. By now though the sedatives only made things worse. Walter entered his nightmare world and the sedatives made it impossible for him to wake. The very thing which was supposed to help, was trapping him in his hell. During the day Walter could function only with the greatest concentration. Sadly Freddy could see that he had reverted, back almost, to when he'd first been admitted. A number of different drug combinations were tried, but none seemed to work. Freddy tried talking to Walter, and although he managed to converse with him, Walter always managed to steer the conversation away from the subjects Freddy wanted to talk about. Walter only wanted to talk about Betty and the time before he went to war. Walter seemed to have become lodged in that time and nothing anyone could do would move him. Freddy decided the best thing to do was to wait. Without the help of Dr George, there was nothing else he could do. Freddy was very disappointed with the way things had turned out. He'd counted Walter as a great success and was hoping to be able to get him home where he would be able to live a normal life. Sadly looking at Walter now as he shuffled about the place he could see this would not happen. He blamed himself; he thought helping the wounded men was the right thing for Walter to do, and at first it had appeared to work, but Walter's mental state had been more fragile than he'd imagined and he'd pushed Walter back inside himself. He just hoped he could pull him back from the brink more quickly this time. He wasn't going to give up on Walter, not after they'd been so close to the cure.

One day, he was sorting through some files pertaining to men treated at the facility towards the end of the war. Freddy wanted everything to be in order now that it looked as if the hospital was to become a Sanatorium again. He noticed a file relating to an Edward Kenneth Campbell. This young man came from the same place as Walter and he'd pushed him around the hospital on more than one occasion while he was under their care. Freddy wondered if they'd talked, and if their talks could have had anything to do with Walter's deterioration. Freddy perused the file and thought he would use some of the information he gleaned from it in their next conversation. He thought if Walter knew the family it might help to reach him again. As he put the file down there was a knock at the door. "Come in," called Freddy. An orderly entered in some agitation.

"Walter's sitting out in the rain, Dr. Pearce. He's near the dovecote and it's pouring. I've called to him from the doorway, but he just ignored me. We thought you ought to know."

Freddy shook his head in exasperation. "I'll get him, Johnson. Leave it with me."

Freddy looked out of the window. He'd been so engrossed in what he'd been doing that he hadn't noticed the change in the weather. When he'd begun his task the sun had been shining, now rain was beating against the window. He wondered that he hadn't heard it. He put on his coat as the rain was torrential, and walked along the corridor to the nearest door leading to garden by the dovecote. He could see Walter sitting on the bench he himself constructed, oblivious to the rain, looking up at the doves sheltering in the cote. As he got closer he could see something was wrong. He quickened his pace and broke into a run. When he reached Walter he knew it was too late. Walter was dead, and had been for some time. The rain ran through Walter's thinning hair and down his face. His clothes were soaking but he would never know. Freddy sat next to him ignoring the pouring rain; and looked up at the doves, probably the last thing Walter ever saw in his life.

"I hope your next life is better than the one you've just had old friend," he said to his silent companion. As he stood to leave, in order to find some stretcher bearers to bring Walter in out of the rain, he saw the envelope sticking out of Walter's inside pocket. He pulled the letter out. As the rain caused the ink to run he saw it was addressed to his parents. He quickly pushed it into his pocket to save further damage, and made his way back inside the hospital. After arranging the removal of Walter's body to the hospital mortuary. Freddy thought about the post-mortem which would have to be carried out. He knew that Walter had just given up. He'd had enough of this life. He couldn't take any more. A post-mortem wouldn't find a broken heart, he thought.

He took the letter into his office to read in private. He opened the envelope; it hadn't been sealed. Inside was a single sheet of paper and on it Walter had written 'more than dead'. Nothing else. Freddy thought back to a conversation they'd had, before Walter had relapsed. They'd been talking about his return from the battlefields and his time on the Belgian farm.

Walter had said, "When men are killed they're dead. There's no coming back. They're gone, and everybody knows it. But me; I came back. I've got a living death. I'm more than dead. I have nothing, can get nothing. Everyone thinks how lucky I am, but I've got nothing to look forward to. Everyone has moved on. Everything I thought I had is gone. How can I get it back? I'm dead; the only difference is that I'm still moving around. The War took it all and then let me come back. I have less than a life. In my eyes I'm just a sightseer, watching other people live. Life goes on around me but I'm not part of it. I'm more than dead." Freddy knew he was talking about Betty and thought at the time he would get over it.

Freddy knew now his parents could never receive a letter from Walter. He could never let them see Walter's last words. It was better left as it was.

Outside Walter's mother's cottage the last petals fell from the rose bushes that would never bloom again.

***

Back in the village life was getting back to normal. Betty was back working at the laundry and Edward was taking on more responsibility at the jewellers as Mr. Cohen talked of retirement. Edward had made a copy of his mother's ring, similar to the one Mr. Cohen had made for her all those years before. He'd made it to test out his dexterity, but also in order to impress his employer. It had done just the opposite.

"There will only ever be one of those rings, while I'm in charge here," he'd said vehemently. "That's your mother's ring. And only hers." He went back to his work, leaving Edward to think over his words. 'Not that close to retirement then", Edward thought grinning to himself, as he looked at his employer stiffly bent over his magnifying glass.

Betty, Naomi and occasionally Audrey still took their stalls to the fairs, which were still popular, although there wasn't as much money about as there used to be. Post-war austerity had started to bite.

Audrey and Betty still made the jams and soups and still dreamed of opening a shop. One day! Maybe!

In the village churchyard at the cenotaph, a simple stone cross made from the local stone. Riven, rough-looking, to symbolise the natural toughness of the local men, and coincidentally, on which a dove regularly roosted. The cross itself stood seven feet high, and was placed on a plinth of four steps, each one foot high. The top plinth bore the legend 'The war to end wars', the monument being raised to honour the fallen from the village, in that war. The plinth below carried all the names of the men lost in that conflict.

The third plinth now carried the names of those lost in WW2, Walter's name, alphabetically, among them. Betty could never bring herself to visit the place. The cenotaph committee were in talks with the stone mason about the possibility of removing the words, THE WAR TO END WARS.